R-T,
MARGARET,
and the
RATS of NIMH

R-T, MARGARET, and the RATS of NIMH

Jane Leslie Conly

illustrations by Leonard Lubin

HarperTrophy®
A Division of HarperCollinsPublishers

R-T, Margaret, and the Rats of NIMH
Text copyright © 1990 by Jane Leslie Conly
Illustrations copyright © 1990 by Leonard B. Lubin
Typography by Joyce Hopkins

Library of Congress Cataloging-in-Publication Data
Conly, Jane Leslie.
  R-T, Margaret, and the rats of NIMH / by Jane Leslie Conly ;
illustrations by Leonard Lubin.
     p.   cm.
  Summary: The further adventures of the intelligent young rat Racso and his friends
Christopher and Isabella as they try to ensure the survival of their secret community
in Thorn Valley after its accidental discovery by two human children.
  ISBN 0-06-021363-9.— ISBN 0-06-021364-7 (lib. bdg.)
ISBN 0-06-440387-4 (pbk.)
  [1. Rats—Fiction.] I. Lubin, Leonard B., ill. II. Title.
PZ7.C761846Rt 1990   89-19968
[Fic]—dc20   CIP
                                                                      AC

First Harper Trophy edition, 1991.

For Will

R-T,
MARGARET,
and the
RATS of NIMH

Chapter 1

"This *might* be it."

Racso, his black beret cocked at a jaunty angle on his furry head, stood staring into the contents of a clay beaker. He took a step backward, forward, to the side, then twirled neatly around in a silent dance. "I mean, Isabella, this really might be it!"

Isabella, a taller rat with curly whiskers, looked skeptical. "This is only the hundredth time you've said that this month, Racso."

"Yeah, but that was before I added the honey-suckle. The honeysuckle makes all the difference."

"It *might* make all the difference, is what you mean." Isabella shook her head in disgust. "I have to go. I'm in charge of dinner tonight."

Racso grinned. "I was hoping you were. And I've been hoping we could have carrots baked with honey, like you made last time."

"Then you should have asked right from the start, instead of acting like you'd made a great discovery."

Racso looked injured. "You should give me the benefit of the doubt. Elvira thinks my potion made Brutus's shoulder heal a lot faster than usual. I saw him by the pond yesterday, and he was hardly limping at all." Brutus had been climbing the mountain trail the month before and had been attacked by a hawk.

Isabella rolled her eyes. "I'll put your picture up beside Louis Pasteur's."

"That's enough! No bickering in the laboratory." An older female rat stood in the doorway.

"Elvira! I thought you were down by the brook, gathering herbs."

"Well, I'm back. And I'd like a little peace and quiet, if you don't mind."

"I've mixed up something new," Racso said quickly. "I added some honeysuckle to the stuff I made last week, and I think. . . ."

"Out!" She brushed his words aside, smiling. "I need to concentrate, and that means being alone."

"You can help me pull up the carrots," Isabella said. "We'll need at least a hundred."

So she *was* going to make his favorite dish! Racso was pleased. As they walked down the central hallway of the rats' huge nest, he couldn't help remembering his first trip down that corridor, almost two years before. He had been a runaway from the big city, tired and scared; and Isabella had scorned him. He'd been afraid to tell her who his father was, because he was afraid she would scorn him even more. Jenner had been one of the super-intelligent rats who'd escaped from the famous laboratories at NIMH and founded their own colony. But Jenner had argued with the other leaders, and had returned to the city an exile. Later he had died a hero sabotaging a dam that would have flooded Thorn Valley. And Racso and the other rats in the sabotage unit had returned as heroes, too. After that, Isabella's attitude toward Racso had changed, and for the better.

"Gonna meet my sweetie tonight. . . ." Racso sang softly. They passed the school—out of session, because it was summer—the meeting room, the nursery, then the many arched doorways that led into the rats' bedrooms. Racso pointed to the door of his own room. Just that morning he'd tacked a piece of birch-bark paper to the wooden door. It was decorated with flowers and hearts drawn with pokeweed ink, and in the center, in fancy lettering, was the message:

Racso
loves
Isabella

Racso had practiced the special curlicues that went on the *a*'s for two days before he'd made the sign, and he was happy with how they'd come out. But Isabella didn't seem as excited as he'd thought she'd be. Instead, she stood there staring at the sign and pulling on her whiskers as if something was bothering her.

"Don't you like it?"

"Uh . . . sure, Racso."

"Did I spell your name wrong or something?"

"No, you got it right. . . ." Isabella hesitated. "But there is something I'd like to talk to you about. . . ."

Racso scowled. That sign was a work of art! She certainly didn't appreciate him the way she should. They entered the dining room, Isabella striding ahead. There were a few rats sharing lunch out of big wooden bowls; Racso guessed that they'd been working somewhere far off and had gotten back late. He noticed his own bowl, with his name engraved on it, near the bottom of a stack of dishes. When he'd first come to Thorn Valley, he'd been appalled by the rats' menu: vegetables, vegetables, vegetables, with here and there maybe a few fruits and nuts mixed in. He'd taught them to make candy, now a favorite treat for the whole community, but for the most part he'd just had to get used to eating their way. Sometimes he still thought about the corner deli on the street where he'd been born. At night he and his friends would sneak under the lunch counter, finding pieces of barbecue potato chips and crumbs from a jelly doughnut.

"Racso!" Isabella tossed him a bag woven out of vines, and took another one for herself. "We ought to be able to fit all the carrots in here." She took a knife from a rack on the kitchen wall. "This is all we'll need—we can cook them outdoors. That'll keep the kitchen from getting too hot."

A moment later they were standing in the big back doorway, flooded with sunlight. Thorn Valley was lovely in summer: The mountainsides were covered with laurel and rhododendron, and the meadows were yellow and pink with clumps of buttercups and wild roses. Directly in front of them a slate walkway bordered by wild geraniums led to the pine grove by the brook. Over to the right were the gardens: square plots filled with beets and turnips and lettuces and cabbages and sweet potatoes and wild asparagus and peppers. Between these were blackberry thickets. There were three walnut trees and a chestnut oak for acorns; sassafras saplings for sassafras tea and root beer; and three large beehives. To the left was the playground the young rats had built with the help of Arthur, the engineer. Racso still loved to slide down the bamboo slide and swing back and forth on the grapevine swing. Down the hill a bit was Emerald Pond. The rats had created it by damming a stream when they moved to the valley four years ago. Now bamboo pipes carried water underground from the pond to the nest and gardens. And just above the pond was the guard tower.

Racso shuddered involuntarily. The guard tower was new. Over the spring two rats had been killed and carried away by a hawk, and two more had been wounded. Now the sky above the gardens was watched continually, and an alarm sounded as soon as the hawk appeared. Everyone had to dive for cover and stay there until it was gone.

"Are you daydreaming?" Isabella gave him a friendly poke. "Is it about me?"

Racso grinned. "Not this time." He didn't want to admit he'd been thinking about the hawk. "What was it you were going to tell me, anyway?"

They had begun walking toward the carrot patch. Isabella looked around to make sure no one else could hear.

"I'm trying to change my image," she whispered.

"What?"

"My image—what the other rats think of me. I'm tired of being plain old Isabella. I want to be thought of as responsible, like Nicodemus or Justin or Hermione. If someone has a problem, I want him to think, Who could give me good advice? Arthur? Elvira? Beatrice? No! ISABELLA!"

Racso stared. He could hardly believe his ears. For Isabella to think that someone would compare *her* to the leaders of the colony! To dream that others would think she had the wisdom of Nicodemus, who had founded Thorn Valley . . . the quick mind of Justin, head of the security forces . . . or the knowledge of the teacher, Hermione. Isabella was a kid, like him!

They arrived at the plot and settled in to work, pulling each carrot, shaking the dirt off, flinging it into the bag.

"But *why* do you want to change your image?" Racso tried to keep his voice casual, as if the idea were entirely sensible.

Isabella hesitated, as if the next admission were a bit embarrassing for her.

"Well, for a couple of years—when I was really young, you know, before I knew any better, that is, I . . ." Isabella shook a carrot hard, as if it had more dirt on it than it really did. "I sort of had a crush on Justin. You had just recently come here, so I don't know if you remember . . ."

"Do I remember!" Racso felt like laughing out loud. "How could I forget! You walked around behind Justin as if you were tied to him with a string. You sat in front of him and tried to get his attention at meetings, and if something needed to be done for him, you always tried to do it first. And you used to go around saying, 'Justin says . . .' as if he were your idol. And you . . ."

"All *right*, Racso!" Isabella threw a carrot so hard that it broke in two. "You don't have to make fun of me!"

"I'm not making fun of you. You asked if I remembered . . ."

"And now I know you do!" Isabella snapped. "Anyway . . ."

"What?"

Isabella pursed her snout. "Well, I think there are rats who might have formed the impression that I was a little . . ." She seemed to be searching for just the right word.

Racso tried to help. "A little . . . dumb?"

"No!"

"Silly?"

"I was not SILLY!" Isabella laid her ears back against her head, a sure sign that she was angry. She worked for a while in silence. She was fast: The carrots followed one another into the bag, one, two, three.

"I was very young back then," she said. "And now and then I let my emotions get the better of me. You might say I was flighty, but I would say that I simply wasn't as mature as I am today."

Racso decided to keep quiet.

"I'm different now," Isabella continued. "Time has mellowed me." Racso was pretty sure they'd read that line in a novel at school, but he nodded. "My judgment has grown sound, and I am ready to share my wisdom. But I fear that the image from years ago might remain in the minds of some rats— those who don't know me well, that is. And the sign you made—though it is very beautiful, Racso, and I love the way you did my name with those curlicues . . ."

"Well?"

"It might remind the others of the *old* Isabella . . . and I wouldn't want that."

"We could ask the others what they think about you," Racso said practically. "We could ask Christopher. I see him right over there, picking blackberries."

"I'd rather wait until I get the chance to improve my image." Isabella thumped another carrot into the bag. "I think we've got about a hundred here." She began to count.

Racso stood quietly. He still got confused when he counted in the high numbers. He waved to Christopher, a whitish rat with a long tail. Christopher waved back. He must have finished his experiment with the solar collector, Racso thought, or else he wouldn't be working in the garden. Christopher despised most jobs. "Too dull!" he always said. Then Racso noticed that for every berry his friend put in the basket, he put another into his mouth! No wonder he'd volunteered to pick blackberries!

"A hundred and fifteen," Isabella finished. "That should be plenty. Now we'll wash them and cut them up . . ."

Racso dragged the two bags over to a place where a bamboo spigot came up from an underground pipe. The shower of water felt good on their paws, and they splashed each other, laughing. They washed each carrot and set it on a pile of straw. The washing created a small river of muddy water, and two baby rats ran up and began to play in it. Their mother, who was working in the parsnips, called to them crossly:

"Seymour! Michaelina! Come back here! It's dangerous to wander away!"

Seymour did run back, but Michaelina darted up to Racso with an impish look in her eyes. She pranced back and forth. "Carrots for supper," she chanted.

"With honey," Racso nodded.

The little rat jumped up and down. "Yum."

"MICHAELINA!"

"Bye-bye," shouted the little rat. She ran away toward her mother. Racso and Isabella laughed.

"What's so funny?" Christopher's berry-stained nose appeared from around the hedgerow. "You two flirting again?"

Isabella stiffened. "No."

"She's trying to change her image," Racso explained. "She wants to be taken seriously."

"Oh." Christopher looked puzzled. "Why?"

"In case I want to become president of Thorn Valley," Isabella said lightly.

Christopher looked as if he'd accidentally swallowed something the wrong way. He coughed several times. Then he said, "Of course."

"Now we need four cups of honey," Isabella said in the same matter-of-fact tone. "And the clay pot from the shelf over the stove."

"We're in luck—here comes Beatrice." A brown rat with delicate features and sharp, sparkly eyes headed toward them. Beatrice was married to Justin and was in charge of the beehives.

"We were just about to come look for you," Racso said. "We need to get some honey."

Beatrice smiled. "And I was just looking for *you*. Elvira thought you'd come out here. We got a letter from the Frisbys—nothing new, really, but I thought you'd like to read it anyway. It's on Justin's desk."

[13]

"I *do* want to." Timothy Frisby, a field mouse who lived with his family on a farm not far from the valley, was Racso's best friend. They'd met when Racso was on his way to Thorn Valley to find the rats. Timothy had discovered that Racso had run away from his home in the city because he wanted to learn to read and write. Since Timothy was traveling to the rats' school, he volunteered to take Racso with him. This year Timothy wasn't coming to school in the valley, though. Instead, he planned to stay on the farm to do experiments with seeds and soil, so that the rats could improve their gardening techniques. Racso missed Timothy already.

"I'll get the honey," Beatrice said. "How much do you need?"

"Four cups will do fine." Isabella was pleased with how efficient and grown-up her voice sounded. Her paws handled the knife skillfully as she sliced each carrot into four pieces.

"Maybe I'll go with you," Christopher said. "I'm bored."

"So bored that you're ready to brave the beehives," Beatrice laughed. "No thanks. Bees do better when they're handled by the same keeper over and over."

"Too bad, Christopher, you can't even get stung when you want to," Isabella said. "But you can make a fire in the outdoor oven for me. And put the clay pot on it, with about two quarts of water inside."

"Oh, I forgot to tell you something." Beatrice came back. "The messenger who brought the letter—a crow—saw a tent in Northwoods, just on the other side of the mountain. But Justin wasn't worried about it. He says humans camp there and go fishing in the stream. They always seem to leave after a few days."

"Watch OUT!" A high-pitched whistle shrieked from the guard tower. The rats dove for cover. From the thorny hedge Racso saw the shadow of wings fall across the garden. He gasped. The baby rat who'd been scampering in the water—Michaelina!—was alone in the turnip plot. The hawk turned sharply, hovered. A large, bony rat dashed from nowhere, flung the baby headfirst into the blackberry bushes, and was gone. The hawk screamed. Racso clung to the brambles with all four paws.

Chapter 2

Crack! Crack! Crack! The feel of the old branch breaking against the solid tree trunk was pleasurable to
the girl, and she held it tight with both hands and
smacked it with all her might. The rotten branch
flew in every direction. One of the pieces banged
against the leg of the folding metal table with a
nice ring; another one hit Arthur right in the small
of the back. He made a sound in between a moan
and a growl, but he didn't look up from where he
was sitting in front of the fire. He had a little metal
tractor in his hands.

"Margaret, you stop banging that stick! You just
hit your brother with it, and it could have hurt

him." Her mother's voice was sharp. "What if it had hit him in the eye?"

"Sorry." Secretly she thought, "If it had hit him in the eye, maybe he would have done something. Maybe he would have stood up and yelled, like any other kid." Margaret was sure that Arthur could talk if he wanted to. She knew that he understood things, even when he pretended he didn't. But he had their mother and dad so worried about him that they didn't know what to do, except to yell at Margaret as if it were her fault.

She hadn't wanted to come camping anyway, but they had made her, saying the idea of a ten-year-old girl staying in the house by herself while the rest of the family was on vacation was just ridiculous. But wouldn't she have had a great time! She and Leon, who lived next door, could have watched TV all day if they'd wanted to. They could have lived on junk food! They could have worn the same clothes every day. They could have made crazy telephone calls to the places with toll-free numbers, like the Swift's Turkey Hot Line and Rubber Duck Baby Pants Company. They could have eaten pizza for breakfast, ice cream for lunch, and M&M's for dinner. She imagined dividing the packages of M&M's into colors, then putting all the browns in one corner of the plate—that would be the meat— and the greens in another—the beans—and then the oranges—carrots. A perfectly balanced meal!

She sighed. Even before the camping trip, her mother had been bugging her. She had taken Margaret aside one day and said, "Maybe the kids won't tease you so much, honey, if you lose a little weight."

Margaret had been furious. "I don't want to look like a stupid Barbie doll!" she'd said.

"Maybe they'll stop calling you names like 'Piano Legs' and 'Creampuff,' " her mom insisted. And for dessert she had cut Margaret a piece of cake so thin that it could hardly stand up by itself.

Margaret kicked her sneaker into a pile of moldy leaves. Camping! She had finished all her comic books, and there wasn't anything left to do. The whole thing was just unfair.

"Margaret!" Her dad's voice drifted down from where he was chopping wood. She began to wander in his direction, winding around trees and thickets as if she were lost inside a maze. Her short brown curls bounced as she walked. She was wearing jeans and a green sweatshirt with a picture of a unicorn on it. She'd picked the sweatshirt out at K Mart last year just before school started.

"I want you to help me carry this wood down, so we can make a big fire." Her father looked a lot like Margaret; his face was more round than square, and he also had curly hair.

"How about letting me chop some wood?" Margaret had asked this once before, and her dad had let her try; but he had been nervous. She guessed he thought she'd accidentally cut her leg off. Then he'd have one kid who couldn't talk and one who couldn't walk. The thought of herself hobbling along on one leg gave Margaret pleasure. She imagined what the other kids in her class would say. Some would be sorry for her, she supposed; others, like Roy Warnell and Elinor Huber, would probably say she had done it just for attention.

To her surprise her dad handed her a hatchet, keeping hold of the handle with one hand. He again showed her how to raise it above her shoulders and bring it down at an angle, to cut a wedge into the yellow pulp of the wood. The wood gave off a pungent smell that tickled her nose. She lifted the hatchet again and again, until at last there was only a thin strip holding the log to the trunk; then he showed her how to push that with her foot until it snapped, and the log fell.

"Good job, Margaret. This locust is hard to cut, but it'll burn a long time."

"Did you learn that when you were in Scouts?"

He nodded. "Sure did. And a lot more, too."

Her father had been a Boy Scout when he was a kid, and he'd loved it. That was when he'd learned to hike and fish and camp. That was one reason he'd thought the camping trip was such a good idea.

She'd tried to tell him that kids were into other things these days—things like hard rock and skateboards and Garbage Pail Kids—but he hadn't really listened. "You don't know what it's like to sleep out under the stars, Margaret," he'd said. "Once you get a taste of the great outdoors, you'll never get it out of your system."

"But what about Artie?" Margaret's mother had sounded worried. Arthur was pale and thin, with fine orangy hair. He had asthma. He had to be taken to the hospital every week for shots. Some of the kids said Arthur was retarded, but the doctors said they couldn't tell for sure.

"It might be the best thing for Artie. I think it'd help him to get out of the house for a while—to see something besides his room and that junk he watches on TV."

And so they'd traded the Buick for Uncle Chris's truck for a week, and Uncle Chris had shown them a map with an old logging road leading into the state forest. And here they were.

"Margaret . . . would you mind watching Artie for a little while? I have a headache, and I thought if I could just lie down for a few minutes, I might be able to get rid of it." Her mom's voice trailed off from inside the tent.

Her father had spent the morning fishing, and had come back to clean the fish and cook them over the fire for lunch. Margaret didn't think she'd like fish, and she'd been certain Arthur wouldn't eat his. Sure enough, he'd sat staring straight ahead until their mom brought him a peanut butter sandwich, the same thing he always had. After lunch their dad had taken the truck into town to get more groceries and some extra fishhooks, and she and Arthur and Mom had stayed at the campsite.

"Margaret, would you mind?" her mother repeated. Her voice sounded tired.

"All right." Margaret really felt like saying, "Quit bugging me!" But she felt a little sorry for her mom, because she hadn't wanted to go camping either. She was a city person who never put on a pair of blue jeans. She took Margaret to museums and concerts, and tried to make her happy. But she worried a lot—especially about Arthur—and she got headaches from worrying.

Margaret knew that she herself would never have any children. When she grew up she planned to have fun all the time, and to do whatever she wanted to, without worrying about anyone else. She planned to make a lot of money on the stock market right away, so she wouldn't have to have a job. She wouldn't be like any of the grown-ups she knew. She was going to be just like she was now, except without anyone to boss her around. And without Arthur!

Arthur was sitting near the ashes of the fire, playing with a toy car. He made it go around and around in a circle, and he would flip it into the air and let it fall. Weird kid! She lifted the lid off the cooler and found a package of raisin cookies. She took three for herself and gave one to Arthur, who dropped the car and clutched the cookie with both hands.

"Margaret, don't eat sweets now. There's fruit if you want it, or diet soda."

Her mother must have heard the rustle of cellophane. Margaret made a face at the tent, took one more cookie, and put the rest back. "Come on, we'll go for a little walk," she said to Arthur in a loud voice.

"Don't go too far, honey," her mother called from inside the tent. This time Margaret didn't even bother to answer. She grabbed Arthur by the arm and pulled him upright. She put his hand in hers and started off. He trotted obediently beside her.

"Now Artie, where would you like to go?"

To her surprise, Arthur didn't ignore the question. Instead he looked around him, up and down the wooded valley, and inclined his head forward, as if pointing in that direction.

"That way?" She watched. Arthur didn't nod but he started walking in the direction he had indicated, so Margaret walked along beside him. She had always thought that Arthur understood more than he let on, and she often tried to test him, to see exactly what he did understand. Sometimes she stood and listened outside the door of his bedroom to see if she could hear him talking to himself.

He had talked some, when he was very small. She remembered he'd said things like "mama" and "dada" and "ball" and had even spoken short sentences like "go out." That was before he got sick. Later he got more and more quiet, until suddenly she noticed that he never talked anymore. And when she mentioned it to her mother, it turned out that she had noticed it a long time ago, and had taken Arthur to a doctor for that, too, but the doctor couldn't do anything about it. Her mother had cried when she told Margaret this, and Margaret had felt mad at Arthur for causing so much trouble.

It wasn't easy having a brother like Arthur. She eyed him appraisingly. He was funny-looking: His wispy hair reminded her of the fluff on a dandelion. And he kept his face fixed in a sort of blank expression, without looking around to see what was going on. Occasionally something seemed to interest him: He loved animals, and he had toys that he played with in his own way, scooting them around on the floor in circles. All the kids said Arthur was weird.

She sometimes complained to her dad about Arthur. "The kids tease me just because of him." Once she said, "He's doing it just to make me unpopular." But her dad shook his head. "Artie is Artie," he had said. "We just have to accept him. If he wants to, one day he'll talk to us. But then again, maybe he won't."

"You don't accept me for what I am," Margaret had argued. "You're always trying to change me."

"You and Arthur are different," her dad said quietly.

She looked around. They were at the crest of a hill: just below them was the old logging road they had followed to get to the campsite. Margaret saw the ruts their truck had made when her dad had turned it around to drive into town. She looked back, over her shoulder. Far away through the trees she could make out a blotch of orange: the tent. Arthur pulled her hand in the opposite direction: toward the logging trail. Margaret hesitated. "I guess we can turn around and follow it back when we need to," she said. "We'll know to go up the hill when we get to the ruts."

They walked a short distance with Arthur leading the way. The road twisted this way, that way; sometimes it seemed to disappear, but then Margaret would see an opening, they would go through, and the track would be there. They saw a blue jay fly in front of them, scolding angrily.

"He must have a nest nearby," Margaret explained. She felt proud of how nice she was being to Arthur. But then she added, "I think we should turn back now—we've been gone quite a while."

Arthur looked disappointed, but they turned around anyway and went back along the track, through an opening, to a place where the path curved around a big thicket. And there, in the middle of the road, was a bear.

Chapter 3

There aren't any bears around here, Margaret thought. Arthur gave her hand a fast, hard jerk. The bear was standing on its hind legs with its mouth open. Margaret was afraid to move, afraid to stand still. In her horror she noticed the quiet shifting of the leaves on the trees, the jay's voice still scolding in the background. She turned and ran, dragging Arthur behind her.

She did not look back. The air was filled with the wild crashing of their flight through the brambles— or was it the bear behind them? Once Arthur tripped and fell, and she pulled him along the ground like a burlap bag filled with stones until he managed to get his feet back under him again. His weight was like a cement block, pulling her back. She wondered if they would both die. She kept going, running through whatever was in front of her, even when the brush looked like a thick wall. She felt as if she were part of a 3-D movie, and she wanted to say, This cannot be real.

She didn't know how long she had been running when she finally looked back and saw nothing but woods and brush and leaves. She dropped to the ground and pulled Arthur down with her. She closed her eyes and listened. The crashing was gone; the only sound was her own panting—a terrible, gasping sound—and Arthur's sobbing.

She looked at Arthur. His face was streaked with tears, and his eyes were wide with terror.

"It's all right, Artie," she said. "It's gone now."

He glanced at her quickly. She wondered if he knew that she was lying, that she had no idea where the bear was or whether it would come back. She wasn't sure how long they lay silently on the ground, holding on to each other until Arthur stopped crying. There was no sound now except the chirping of birds and the wind rustling the leafy canopy of the trees.

"Maybe we should stand up," Margaret said finally. She got up on her hands and knees, then all the way. Her legs trembled, and she had to make a conscious effort to steady them by putting her weight first on one, then the other. She grasped Arthur by the arm and pulled him up, too. He let his legs collapse, so that she was holding his full weight. She tried it again, and he did the same thing.

"All right," she said. "I'll leave you here by yourself."

For a moment she thought that Arthur was actually going to speak. He opened his mouth in the shape of the word *no*, and his blue eyes overflowed with tears. Slowly he got up on all fours, then grabbed the pocket of Margaret's jeans and pulled himself to his feet. He stood there stiffly, as if he were made of wood.

"We'll go this way," Margaret said. "This is the way we came."

They walked back through the woods, skirting the heavy underbrush. There were places where the leaves seemed to be pushed around, as if someone had come running through; at first, Margaret thought they formed a sort of trail, but later there seemed to be so many paths that she decided they must have been made by the wind. She transferred Arthur's hand from her pocket to her hand and held it tight. Although she couldn't be sure, she was pretty certain she was heading in the right direction, and she thought the logging road should appear at any moment.

They walked and walked. Margaret remembered from school that there was a way to tell direction by the location of the sun. She stopped and checked: It was over her left shoulder, dropping almost even with the treetops. Did that mean the west was to her left? Where had the sun been this morning? It had been shining through the window of the tent onto her face; she had come out and it had been behind the tent as she faced it: east. But what direction had they taken on the walk? West, of course, and when they had turned right on the logging road that would have been north. Meaning that they should head southeast to get back to the campsite? That would be away from the sun—which was the direction they were walking—and perhaps a little more to the right. But to the right there were pine trees, and Margaret was sure she hadn't seen those before.

The ground began to slope upward. They had come over a hill when they first started walking, so for a moment Margaret thought they must be very close to the tent. She had the idea that if she could reach the top of the hill, she would be so high up that she could look down and see the campfire and the tent. And so she hurried, pulling Arthur along by the hand. The ground remained steep, but there did seem to be a small path up the hillside.

By now the sun had slipped below the tree line, so that the light was filtered and the air was cooler.

Margaret was confused. She kept going over the directions in her mind: they had come west, then north; then they had seen the bear, and run off . . . which way? They were heading east, which must be right. Yet everything looked unfamiliar. And she was sure the hill they'd crossed on the way hadn't been nearly this steep.

Arthur moaned. Margaret looked down at him. She'd been concentrating so hard she'd almost forgotten about him. Probably it had been hard for him to keep up. Soon it would be twilight. The chances of finding the tent at dusk didn't seem good.

She decided to let Arthur rest for a minute, and sat down with him on a mossy stone. He still looked scared. "We're on our way back to the tent, Artie, and when we get there we'll have supper . . . maybe hot dogs and beans, or hamburgers," she tried to reassure him. But Arthur didn't seem to be listening, and hearing herself, Margaret felt frightened and alone. She felt like shouting, I'M LOST! But she couldn't, because of Arthur.

She wondered if her parents were looking for them. Her mom had been almost asleep when they left, and she had no idea how much time had gone by since then: several hours, at least. And her dad had been in town. The shopping might take him a long time.

"Are you feeling better, Artie? Ready to go on?"

She kept her voice cheerful, as if they were doing something fun. She thought briefly of Leon: Wait until he heard about this! He'd probably say she'd made the whole thing up—especially the part about the bear!

The bear . . . with a shiver Margaret looked around. But the woods were quiet. She pulled Arthur to his feet. His hand felt as limp as a rag. They began walking up the hill. Sometimes it was so steep that Margaret had to stand behind Arthur and boost him over rocks. She no longer told herself that they would find the campsite anytime now; instead, she held on to the idea that when she got to the top of the hill, she would be able to see smoke from the fire. They came to a patch that was all rock; they had to climb over it on their hands and knees. When they'd reached the end Margaret turned and looked back. She gasped. Spread out to her right were thousands of tiny trees, and behind them the orange ball of the setting sun. The view to her left was obscured by a rock shelf that jutted into the air at an odd angle. She searched the forest for a trail of smoke, but there was nothing.

She sat down on the nearest rock. They were lost, and it was getting dark. She imagined Leon saying, "And of all the people to be stuck with, your little brother." But there was nothing funny about it. She bit her lip to keep from crying. Arthur looked up at her, his eyes round. She felt as if they were the only two people left in the world. What would become of them? And it was all her fault; she should never have gone so far from the tent. She imagined her mother's face, her mouth open, calling their names. If only she could hear her voice, or feel her mother's arms around her. But instead the silence seemed to form a circle around them, as if nothing—no person, no sound—could get in.

"We'll have to go on," she said out loud. "There's nothing else to do. We'll have to try and find somebody." She remembered her dad saying that the state forest included thousands of acres of wilderness. "We're lost, Artie," she said in a weak voice.

Arthur began to cry again.

"Don't do that," Margaret said. "It won't help."

To her surprise Arthur stopped. He rubbed his sleeve against his face, then stood up stiffly and held out one hand. They began walking up the hill. They walked until it was dark. They reached a part of the hill where there were no more trees, only stone. Then suddenly Arthur stumbled. Margaret saw that he was walking with his eyes almost closed. She picked him up under the arms. He wasn't heavy, and the stone under her feet was smooth and flat. She carried him that way for fifty yards, then laid him down and rested herself. She felt numb. She picked Arthur up and carried him a bit farther, then rested again.

It was funny—she didn't feel tired. She was scared—more scared than she had ever been—but at the same time, she felt clearheaded and steady. She thought about the day, how it had started out with all of them waking up in the tent, eating cereal, the fishing trip, the walk, the bear . . . and now this. It had been the longest day of her whole life. And she might die, and Arthur might die. She glanced at him, lying curled on his side, fast asleep. She had never liked him much, had simply thought of him as someone to be put up with. But now they were stuck with each other. She decided she would save him if she could.

After that, she felt a little better. It was as if there were a reason for things to turn out okay. She picked him up, carrying him draped over her two arms the way someone carries a baby. Her stocky legs pumped steadily up the hillside. Now and then she stopped, laid him down, and rested. He slept heavily, without stirring.

Sometime later—how much later she wasn't sure—she reached the crest of the hill. She put Arthur down and looked back the way she had come. In the moonlight she saw the shapes of trees, spreading as far as she could see. It was too dark to see anything else. The night had grown cool, and the air became a fine, thin mist.

She had to find a place for them to sleep. She

searched among the rocks, crossing a sort of natural walkway and then descending. She found a dark opening between stones: a cave. Inside, it was dry. From the side of the rock by the entrance grew a small pine tree. She put Arthur down, crawled inside, and pulled him in after her. The ground smelled musty, like old pine needles.

She curled up to sleep. It was only then—just as she was about to close her eyes—that she remembered Arthur's medicine.

Chapter 4

It was Racso who saw the courier approaching. At first he thought it was the hawk. He flung himself into a honeysuckle thicket and lay trembling on the ground, waiting for the alarm to sound. But it didn't, and after a bit he peeked out. A large crow was circling over the front door of the nest, a paper in its beak. Racso climbed out of the thicket and signaled for the courier to drop the letter. He ran zigzagging past the door to try to catch it in his mouth. He almost did, but the letter was swept up out of his reach by a gust of wind. Christopher saw it and got into the act himself.

"Hey, it's mine!" Racso was irritated.

"Too bad." Christopher was taller and faster than Racso. He gave a mighty leap and ended up with the envelope clutched firmly between his jaws.

"You give it back!" Racso grabbed the other half of the letter in his mouth. "I saw it first!"

Christopher shook his head firmly. Racso refused to let go and the letter ripped a little bit. He tried to hit Christopher with one paw. He stretched his toenails out and tried to scratch him. He was thinking, I won't really hurt him, but I was the one who . . .

"*Ouch!*" Christopher spit the letter out and grabbed his side. There was a pink line that Racso's toenail had made in the light fur. Racso started to pick up the letter but was stopped by a smart blow from Christopher's tail, right across his nose. It really stung! He fought back tears. What kind of friend was Christopher, anyway?

"Hey there, fellows." A deep voice made them both jump. "Who is that letter addressed to?" An older rat with silvery fur and a black eye patch stood in the doorway. He carried a bent hickory twig to help him walk. His face was stern.

"To Justin." Racso was embarrassed. He wondered how much of the incident Nicodemus had seen. He was mad at Christopher—this was all his fault. "It's a little bit torn," he added lamely.

Nicodemus bent over with some effort and picked

the letter up. "Go get Justin, both of you. Curious," he muttered to himself. "We had another letter from Timothy just this week."

Justin came out and nodded deferentially to Nicodemus. "How are you feeling today?"

"Not bad." But Nicodemus couldn't help wincing as he shifted his weight from one paw to the other. He handed the letter to Justin. Justin tried to piece the birchbark together where it had ripped, but there was a jagged tear that left a wide-open space. " 'Hi, two . . . lost in Northwoods . . .' " Justin squinted. "Some is missing here . . . let's see, 'they have a heli . . .' I can't get that word, either." He looked annoyed. "This is really smudged, besides being torn. Did you all keep it in your mouths while you were fighting over it? The ink is smeared!"

"Let me see." Nicodemus bent over the paper. " 'They have a heli . . . copter.' A helicopter!" He looked up at Justin quickly, then bent over the letter again. " 'They do not plan to cross the mountains but . . . Love, Timothy.' "

"When's it dated?"

"About an hour ago."

"I'm going to go in and turn on the radio," Nicodemus said. "Maybe you'd better come with me."

"What about us?" Racso asked. He felt a little hurt. After all, he had seen the crow before anyone else.

"We'll let you know if we hear anything," Justin said. And he and Nicodemus went inside without looking back.

Racso made a face at the door where the two older rats had disappeared. "We'll let you know . . ." he mimicked. "That wasn't very nice of them, was it, Christopher?"

Christopher was scowling, too. "Sometimes I think they don't appreciate us enough around here, you know?" He sat back on his hind legs. "Anyway, what's a helicopter?"

"It's kind of like an airplane, but it's shaped like a tadpole with a little whirligig on top. At least that's what I remember . . . it's been a long time since I've seen one."

Christopher's eyes brightened. "You mean it flies?"

"That's right, but not as high as a plane. I think the thing on top is called a propeller."

Christopher had picked up a twig and was twirling it slowly. "So it uses a motor to turn the blade, right? And the displaced air . . ."

"I don't *know* how it works," Racso interrupted.

"I think I could build one, if I had the right materials," Christopher said, more to himself than to Racso. "And then I could fly wherever I wanted to."

"Like where?"

"Oh, I don't know . . . China, maybe."

"China!" Racso hooted. "That's halfway around the world! You'd have to fly over the *ocean* to get to China! Why, you'd have to build a helicopter that could fly over the mountain, over Northwoods, over Timothy's farm, over the countryside, over the city. . . ." He shook his head. "You don't have any idea how far that is. *I* do, because I came all the way from the city when I ran away and traveled to Northwoods and met Timothy and—"

"Came to the valley," Christopher finished. He was still playing with the twig. "And you're happy because you have your best friend Timothy—even though he isn't here right now—and you have Isabella and you have Elvira to teach you stuff in the lab. So you have everything you want."

"Not *everything*. I'd like to have more candy and some remote-control cars . . . and maybe a new hat." Racso took off his beret and looked at it. There was a hole in the back where he'd torn it on a sharp branch. "A new hat would be nice."

Christopher sighed. He threw the twig high up in the air and watched it come down. Then he threw it up again. Racso watched him.

"Why do you want to go to *China*?"

"I'd just like to see what other places look like. I've never been outside the valley. I've never even seen a cow, or a donkey, or a cat."

"Cats are mean." Racso bared his teeth and held

his front paws up menacingly. "They look like this, except they're bigger and more furry. And they try to creep up on you and grab you with their sharp claws." He jumped on Christopher and tickled him. "Let's play," he said. "I don't feel like going back to the lab right now."

"Want to go swimming?"

"Nope."

"Sneak some candy from the storeroom?"

"Nope."

"Take a hike?"

"Oh—I guess so."

So they packed some food and went off together.

A few minutes after they left, Justin announced a meeting indoors in twenty minutes. Rats came hurrying from the fields, the garden, the stream, and from inside the nest, too: from the kitchen, the infirmary, the lab. "What's it about?" "Don't know." "Short notice, isn't it?" Rats sprawled on the floor and lounged against the walls and beside the big arched window. Justin, Nicodemus, and Hermione sat in front. Hermione called the meeting to order. Then Nicodemus himself stepped forward.

"I got a letter from Timothy Frisby this afternoon alerting us that there are human children lost in Northwoods. They wandered away from their camp and are missing."

Isabella sat bolt upright. Missing children! And not that far away, either! Maybe this would be her chance to show the other rats how she'd changed! Maybe she could be a leader in the search! She turned to look at Racso and Christopher, to see if they were thinking the same thing she was.

But they were nowhere to be seen.

Chapter 5

Margaret didn't wake up all at once. Instead she lay there with her eyes closed, hugging her arms tight against her for warmth. Near her she could hear soft breathing: Arthur. Her mother and father were somewhere else. Where? She shifted and turned. There was a funny smell on the floor: a musty, acrid smell. She was not in the tent. Her hands came up and rubbed her eyes, and she opened them just as she remembered: She was in a cave, and Arthur was with her. It wasn't a dream, because they were here together. And alone.

They were lost. She had the impulse, as she had the night before, to scream, Help us! Help us! Instead she sat up and looked around. The door of the cave—a jagged opening about a foot across—was close by, and she could see that it was daylight outside. But most of the cave was in shadow. She could just make out the rough contours of the walls, which sloped gradually back until they met in a triangle about ten feet behind where Arthur was sleeping.

She crawled to the door and looked out. There was a stunted pine tree growing out of a crack in the rock wall just to the right. On the other side she could see small bushes and more rock. She glanced at Arthur; he was sleeping peacefully. She clambered out the door and stood up.

The sun was partway up in the sky, as if it might be late morning. The hillside was littered with rocks: big ones and little ones, with bushes growing in between them. Just a little way down was a black-berry bush. She was starving! She hurried down and began to eat. The berries were sweet and juicy, and for a while she forgot about being lost and only remembered being hungry.

She picked extra berries for Arthur and carried them back to the cave in the fold of her sweatshirt. He was still asleep. She put them in a little pile beside the entrance, then sat down cross-legged on a flat rock to think. She had no idea where they were, but it didn't look anything like the woods where the campsite was. She was afraid that if they tried to find the camp, they would get even more lost. Surely their parents were looking for them by now. Maybe she could make a sign to show them they were here.

That's what she would do! She found a stick and scratched HELP US in huge letters in a dirt bank below the blackberry bush. Then she found a piece of sharp stone, and used that to scratch the same message on the side of a large rock above the cave. She piled up some stones in a pyramid to call attention to it.

She decided to sit on a ledge near the cave and wait to be found. She folded her legs underneath her and made her back very straight. She tried calling out loud: "MOM! DAD! We're over here!" She did this about twenty times. There was no reply. She thought grimly of all the times she dreamed of a world without parents, without any adults at all. When they'd been around they'd always seemed to be in the way: Can't do this; do that; hurry up; it's time for school. But to be lost in the wilderness with Arthur! She felt as lonely as a speck of dust floating in the darkness of outer space. It was as if she and Arthur had landed on another planet.

Racso couldn't really forgive Christopher for ripping the letter, even though he knew he should.

For one thing, Timothy was *his* best friend, not Christopher's, and the letter was from Timothy. For another, it was cruel of Christopher to take advantage of the fact that Racso was short for his age. And Christopher definitely had taken advantage, for he had jumped just beyond Racso's reach to grab the letter as it was falling. And Christopher might not mind getting in trouble with Nicodemus, but Racso *did* mind. He remembered his teacher Hermione had once referred to him in front of the other pupils as "sensitive." That was a good word for him: sensitive. Christopher could be a bully if he wanted to, but that didn't mean that Racso was going to like it. Anyway there were plenty of rats around to be friends with, rats with other things to do besides hurting the feelings of those who were supposed to be their good friends.

They reached a steeper part of the path. Christopher went first, and Racso could just see the end of his tail as he rounded the bend up front. Racso was puffing from exertion. A minute later Christopher's face peered down at him from a stone ledge above the trail.

"Here's a good spot, Racso. Are you ready for our picnic?"

"Sure." Racso answered as if he didn't feel grumpy, even though he did. He scrambled up onto the flat rock and checked the sky for the hawk: all clear. Christopher took the provisions out of his knapsack: two corn muffins left over from breakfast, a carrot, a turnip, and a piece of honeycomb wrapped in a cabbage leaf.

"You can almost see Emerald Pond from here." Christopher nodded off to the left and downhill.

Racso hadn't realized how hungry he was. He crammed a muffin into his mouth, then the raw carrot before Christopher had even turned around. Next he started on the honey. He knew he was really only entitled to half the honey, but Christopher wasn't looking, and the honey was so good. . . .

"Hey! What happened to all the food?"

"There's a muffin left for you, and some honey." Racso took the remaining piece of honey, about the size of a matchstick, out of his paw and set it back in the center of the cabbage leaf. He was suddenly aware that the honey looked very small and the cabbage leaf very large.

"But I brought a *big* piece." Christopher looked hard at Racso.

"I ate about half of it, and I put the rest back."

"But that's not a fraction of what I brought!"

"I think it's more than a fraction," Racso said hesitantly. "I think—"

"WHERE IS IT?"

"I ate it," Racso said quickly. "Because it was your fault about the letter."

"WHAT? What are you talking about?"

"You jumped up higher than I could, just because you're taller," Racso said. He was aware that this sounded lame, but he kept going. "And I think that was wrong, because—"

"SHUT UP!" Christopher screamed. His ears were flat against his head. He flung the cabbage leaf into the dirt, stuffed the muffin into his knapsack, and strode away without looking back.

Racso sat quietly. His feelings were a little hurt, but he *had* gotten most of the honey, and he'd also let Christopher know how he felt about the letter. Hermione always said it was better to be honest about your feelings. Anyway, he hadn't felt like climbing much higher. He would make up with Christopher later. Maybe he would even apologize for eating most of the honey. Or make something special for Christopher. With that thought he began to climb down the mountain path.

Christopher couldn't remember when he'd felt so disgusted! It was just like Racso to make up some stupid excuse for eating the honey. If Christopher hadn't turned around in time, he would have eaten it all. Christopher kicked a stone that was lying in the path, then another. Racso would be sorry! He'd find out what happened when you played a trick like that on Christopher!

Christopher was so mad that he wasn't particularly

watchful as he trotted up the trail, then across the stone walkway to a spot where a bent pine tree was growing out of a crack in the rock. Beside the tree was the opening to his secret hideout. He slipped in quickly and stood in the half light, breathing deeply. Then he stopped breathing. His eyes opened wide in their sockets and every hair on his body stood on end. A pair of eyes stared directly into his. A huge, pale face surrounded the eyes; below them, a mouth opened and closed, as if it were trying to speak but could not.

Chapter 6

Christopher stared. The face was a foot away from him, hanging just a few inches above the floor of the cave. His legs felt glued to the ground, but his mind raced. Snatches of a song his mother once sang came to him suddenly: "Remember the man in the moon. . . ." But in school Hermione had said the moon was big, and thousands of miles away.

It was alive, Christopher felt sure of that. Its eyes were open very wide, as if it, too, were frightened, and its face was streaked with dirt. As his eyes adjusted to the dark, Christopher could see that there was more of it, and that it had been lying down. He saw pale arms, hands, fingers; stretching beyond the head was a body that ended in two legs. He took a sharp breath. Could it be human?

He had seen people once, almost two years ago, when men were trying to build a dam at the north end of the valley. That fall two explorers had come from the Trout River up the creek in a metal canoe. Christopher had been near the top of a pine tree overlooking the creek when he spotted them; he'd been so fascinated that he'd tried to climb out on a thin branch to get a better look. But the branch had broken, throwing him to the ground in a terrible accident. His injuries had healed slowly. Lying in his bed in the infirmary, he had tried to remember the humans' faces, but the memory was a blur mixed with pine branches and sky.

He decided to retreat. He lifted his front paw slowly and moved it back, then moved his hind paws one at a time. He felt the warm sun on his tail as it slid out the cave door. The other creature was still. He continued to back up slowly, until his hindquarters were out, then his shoulders. The eyes in the round face looked less frightened, as if they realized he was leaving. Christopher felt a strange bond with those eyes. They stared at each other until Christopher was outside.

Back in the sunlight, he looked around to make sure no one had seen him. There were only the bent pine tree and the rock wall. On impulse he reached into his knapsack, took out the corn muffin, and set it in the doorway. Then he scurried to the closest thicket and hid himself.

He had been right to leave, for ten minutes later another one came. This time there was warning: the noise of a heavy weight slipping and sliding, a drawing in and out of breath, and a voice speaking, saying something that sounded like "R-T." Then it appeared. It was larger, with dark hair and a broad face. Its body was muscular, with thick legs, and it was wearing a green garment with a picture of a horse on it. Christopher felt sure this one *was* human. He was so excited that he trembled. It began to speak.

"R-T, I'm sorry that I left you for so long, but I had to figure out what to do, and I thought you were still asleep. I left some blackberries for you . . ." As the big one turned to get the berries, the small human appeared in the doorway and grabbed the muffin. It shoved the whole thing in its mouth. The other one saw it chewing.

"What are you eating? Didn't you hear me say I had some berries?"

R-T didn't answer.

"Don't pick up things off the ground and eat them, no matter how hungry you are. That's dangerous. They might be poisonous or something." And it handed over the berries, which R-T shoved in his mouth. He chewed and swallowed, chewed and swallowed, as if he'd been half starved.

He! Christopher couldn't be sure why he'd decided the little person was male and the big one female, but he was certain of it. And she was in charge.

Now R-T was sitting, and she was talking to him, explaining something.

"I've put up some signs, and I know they're looking for us," she said. "We have food and water. We'll just stay here until they find us. It shouldn't be long—maybe a day or two. It'll be an adventure for us, like Robinson Crusoe or something."

So they were lost. Christopher felt a chill run down his spine. They were lost, and he was the only one who knew.

"Maybe they'll end up making a movie about us," the girl continued. "Then we'll make a lot of money, and be rich. And I'll be able to get a stereo—a really good one—and I'll have soundproofing put up on the walls, so I can play it loud."

Christopher shifted uneasily in the thicket. He should tell the other rats, of course. There were two humans in the valley, and from the sound of it, there might soon be more. And that meant danger for the rats: They might be discovered. They could lose the nest and gardens, and their identity might be uncovered, too. Christopher shivered. He didn't want to tell. The truth was, the moment he'd seen R-T in the cave had been the most exciting moment of his whole life, and he didn't want to share it.

"He's my secret," he muttered to himself. "Mine."

He watched over the children until it was dark, when they went into the cave to sleep. He decided to make his bed in the same thicket where he'd been hiding. But he needed food. At the nest he could get food for R-T, too. He'd have to sneak it from the storeroom, but night was a good time for sneaking: He and Racso often raided the barrels of raisins and peanuts right before bedtime. Racso! He'd forgotten all about their fight.

Christopher scurried down the mountainside, skidding around corners and leaping the small rocks that were in his way. He couldn't waste a second! He hit the front door without slowing down, raced through the corridor, and screeched around the corner to the storeroom. No one was there! Quickly he chose supplies that he thought the boy would like: carrots, walnuts, raisins, honey, three thick slices of Isabella's acorn bread. He wrapped these in birch-bark paper and shoved them into his knapsack. So far, so good!

Now to his bedroom. . . . He couldn't believe the nest was so quiet; he hadn't met a soul. The room was the same mess he'd left that morning: books scattered across the bed; a pile of acorn shells beside them, left over from his midnight snack; a purple spot on the reed rug where he'd spilled most of his bottle of pokeberry ink. Pieces of a game of checkers he and Racso had played on Tuesday were still on a little makeshift board beside the arched window. He grabbed his blanket and tied it to the bottom of the knapsack. Then he raced through the front door and off.

Back at the thicket, he stowed his supplies, then crept to the door of the cave. The girl's breathing was heavy, reminding him of the groaning of old rope when they pulled a bucket of water from the well. He had to stand there for a minute before he heard the boy at all. His faint intake of breath was half sigh, half gasp. But he was there. Christopher went back to the thicket, untied his blanket, and went to sleep.

The girl didn't come to the doorway until the sun was over the cliff on the east side of the valley. Then she crawled out, looking stiff and unhappy. She was even dirtier than she'd been the day before— her hair was covered with dried pine needles, and there was a brown smudge across one cheek. She glanced back once, then clambered slowly down the slope to the blackberry bush.

This was his chance! Christopher grabbed the knapsack and scooted inside the cave. The boy was asleep on his stomach, one hand under his cheek. Christopher took out the packets of food and laid them beside the boy's head. He longed to touch R-T's fine orangy hair, to see what it felt like; but just then R-T shifted in his sleep, groaning. The girl could be back at any moment. Christopher wanted to be certain that R-T got a chance to eat. He looked like he needed it! He reached out and touched the boy's face lightly with his paw. The eyelids fluttered, then opened. Christopher ran out the door.

None too soon. He heard the girl stumbling up from the rocks below. She had turned up her shirt like an apron and filled it with berries. She sat down near the cave and piled half the berries beside her. She ate the rest, jamming them into her mouth as if she didn't care how they tasted. When she finished, she looked around in every direction, as if she hoped to see something she hadn't seen before.

Then R-T appeared in the doorway. In one hand he held the packets of food; in the other, a half-eaten slice of acorn bread.

"You're awake . . ." It took her a minute to see the tiny slice of bread. Then she seemed to swell with excitement.

"Let me see that!" She made a grab for it, but he shoved it quickly in his mouth and swallowed without chewing. Good for you, Christopher thought.

"ARTHUR!" She loomed above him. Her large hand reached out, wresting the packets from him.

She opened them, her hands shaking. Silently she observed the little portions of food: the nuts, raisins, carrots, the honey still on the comb, the two remaining slices of bread.

"Where did you find these?"

He pointed inside the cave. She took him by the arm and went inside, but after a minute they came back. She knelt down and examined the food again, poking it cautiously with one finger. She ate one of the raisins, took a bite of carrot.

"Arthur." She put her hands on the boy's shoulders and stared at him. "Did you see someone bring this food?"

He shook his head. He was angry. He was sure the food had been put there for him.

"Arthur!" Her voice was stern. "You have to answer."

But he wouldn't answer. He thought vaguely of the animal. He'd seen it leaving the cave again, just as he woke up. It reminded him of a squirrel, except that its tail was thin and pink. He was sure it had brought the food. But it was supposed to be his: a present. And he was so hungry! He pointed to his mouth and began to cry.

She set the food in front of him, taking only a small amount for herself. "I know you're hungry," she said more gently. "But we've got to find out who brought it!"

Chapter 7

Someone knew.

Margaret watched Arthur eat. In one hand she held the packets in which the food had been wrapped. They were paper, cut into rectangles about the size of candy-bar wrappers. The paper had an odd consistency—it was slightly brittle, and was colored light brown. She examined each piece, front and back, thinking there might be writing on it. But there wasn't.

Someone knew.

Part of her felt like shouting for joy. But it was so confusing. Had the person seen her signs and brought the food to the cave? If so, why hadn't he come forward and introduced himself? Where was he now? Had he called the police or her parents? Her head whirled. She ate half of one of the little pieces of bread. The flavor was nutty; odd, but good. But she wanted more: It was such a little piece. I could easily eat the whole loaf, she thought.

Perhaps the person was still close by. She began to shout: "HELLO." "WHERE ARE YOU?" "PLEASE COME BACK!" There was no reply. She looked for footprints, but the ground outside was rocky, and inside the dusky cave she couldn't find any distinct print.

Arthur had finished his meal and was watching her. She had a funny feeling that he knew more than he was letting on. He had been in the cave when the food was left, though he might have been sleeping. But he seemed calm, as if he expected that someone would look after them. He had gone without his medicine for two days, yet his breathing seemed almost normal. She mustn't upset him. But she was determined to find out what he knew.

She remembered a game her parents played with Arthur, when they were trying to help him communicate. They would hold up little cards one at a time, and ask him to clap when he saw whatever they wanted him to identify: a triangle, or the color blue, or a picture of a girl. If Arthur was in a good mood, he liked the game, and played it pretty well; but if he was in a bad mood, he wouldn't clap at all, not even to get a piece of candy.

It was worth a try. She sat down opposite him. "We're going to try to figure out who brought the food," she said, trying to make her voice light-hearted. "I'll say something, and if you know it's true, clap your hands. If you don't know, don't clap. Understand?"

Arthur nodded.

"The person who brought the food is a man," said Margaret.

Arthur waited.

"The person who brought the food is a woman."

Nothing. Still, Arthur's eyes were bright, as if he were waiting for the right clue.

"The person is a child."

Nothing. Margaret was starting to feel discouraged.

"The person was wearing blue jeans."

Nothing.

"The person was wearing a knapsack."

Arthur stared. There had been a knapsack each time, he was certain of it. He wasn't sure whether to clap or not, so he brought his hands together softly, just once.

"He was wearing a knapsack!" Margaret tried to

keep the urgency out of her voice. Arthur did know something! "He was wearing a knapsack, right, Artie?"

Again Arthur paused, but brought his hands together softly. She hadn't asked about the animal, and the animal was important. If she asked about that, he would clap loud.

"Was it a woman? Clap if it was a woman!"

Arthur waited.

"A man? A kid, like us?"

Arthur looked confused. She wasn't asking the right questions.

"It's got to be one of them!" Margaret's mind raced. Maybe for some reason Arthur didn't know the sex of the person. But he might know something else.

"Which way did he go? Arthur, did he go that way?" She pointed down the slope, toward the blackberry thicket. "Clap if he went that way."

Nothing. Arthur couldn't remember which way it had gone, he wasn't sure he'd even noticed.

"Did he go that way?" She pointed up, beyond the rocky ledge. But again Arthur did nothing, just sat there.

Margaret felt anger rising in her throat. Surely he knew! He knew, but he was being stubborn, just the way he was at home. He knew, but he wouldn't say.

"Arthur!" She made her voice strong. "You have to tell me. It's very important!"

Arthur put his hands behind his back.

"You have to tell me! I need to know!"

He just sat.

"If you don't tell me I'll go away! I'll leave you here by yourself!"

Arthur stared. Behind his back his fingers curled around and touched each other. She had wanted to play the game, but she hadn't asked the right questions. And now she was angry at him. He felt as if he'd swallowed something too big for his throat. He watched as she got up and walked deliberately away. A tear rolled down his cheek, into his mouth. Then he realized he was going to have the problem. He felt like all the breath was being squashed out of him. He imagined his mother coming with the tube, but she didn't come. He lay down on the rock, gasping, nothing else in his mind.

Christopher watched from the thicket. He had seen rats suffer attacks like this, where they panted and gasped for breath. Sometimes they came out of it on their own. Other times they swallowed a green potion that Elvira or Racso prepared for them. The potion slowed their breathing, and their reactions, too; they must lie still for a full hour after drinking it. Christopher wasn't sure whether the potion would help R-T. The boy was stretched flat, head to one side. He had stopped gasping but his breathing was fast and light. He could die, Christopher thought. I'm the only one who knows he needs help. Without me, he could die.

He went over and stood beside Arthur. This time Christopher didn't think about what he *should* do, or what would be best for the rest of the rats. He spoke.

"Don't be scared. You're going to be okay."

Arthur's eyes flicked open.

"Down at the nest we have medicine that could help you," Christopher continued. "I'm going to get some for you, and more food, too. Is there anything else you need?"

Arthur just stared.

"I already know you're called R-T—I heard the other one call you that." Christopher paused and looked around. "She really shouldn't have left you here the way she did. But I'll take care of you. And I suppose she'll come back, anyway."

A part of him wished she *wouldn't* come back, but he didn't say that.

Arthur groaned. He wanted Margaret.

"Do you want to come with me? Is that what's wrong?"

Arthur shook his head: no. He didn't want to go without Margaret.

[64]

"Believe me, I'll come back," Christopher said. He slipped on his knapsack and nodded good-bye. "My name is Christopher," he said. He set off down the trail at a fast clip.

Margaret came back as soon as the animal had gone. She had been hiding. She didn't look angry anymore, but she stared at Arthur as if he looked different. For a minute she didn't say anything. Then she said, "I saw it, Artie."

He looked at her.

"The thing with the knapsack," she said. "It looked like a rat. And it was talking to you."

She sat down heavily. Tears rolled down her cheeks, but she didn't bother to wipe them away.

Chapter 8

Food and medicine. The words beat a rhythm in Christopher's brain as he raced down the trail. He was worried about R-T—very worried—and he had to get the medicine right away. So he was almost all the way to the nest before the thought struck him: I talked to him! I talked to R-T!

There were going to be problems, he could see that already. Whatever food he brought for the boy would have to be shared with the female. That meant he would need a lot of food. And sneaking the medicine wasn't going to be that easy. For one thing, he wasn't sure which of the potions was which, and he didn't want to give R-T the wrong thing.

For another, there was almost always somebody in the lab, either Elvira or Racso.

Racso. Christopher's legs kept racing but his mind slowed, considering. Racso would keep the secret. And Racso had lived in the city most of his life, so he knew a lot about humans. If anyone at Thorn Valley could give him good advice about R-T, it would be Racso.

Christopher found Racso in the laboratory. He made sure they were alone. He closed the door to the corridor and pulled him into a corner. "Listen," he whispered, "I have to tell you something. And you have to keep it a secret."

"I've been wondering where in the world you *were*! Everybody's been working to camouflage the gardens because of the missing children, and you haven't even been around."

Christopher had been trying to frame the words he would say next, so he wasn't really listening to Racso, but he couldn't help hearing the words "missing children." He scowled impatiently. "What are you talking about? Did some of the little rats wander away?"

"Not little rats!" Racso was pleased to be the one to break the news. "Human beings!"

Christopher's jaw dropped.

"They got lost on the other side of the mountain,

and people are looking for them with *helicopters*.
Nicodemus and Justin said they might fly over the
valley, so we had to cover up the gardens and take
down all the play equipment until the search is over.
I found out about it when I got back from our hike.
We worked until past midnight. Where were you?"
Racso asked.

Christopher took a deep breath. "I found them,"
he said.

They would have kept it a secret between themselves, except Racso argued that they would never
be able to sneak enough food on their own, or carry
it up the mountain to feed the humans. Think as
they might, there didn't seem to be any way around
that. Racso maintained that the larger child would
eat three pounds of food a day, and the small one
probably one pound. Between himself and Christopher they might carry close to two and a half pounds,
but that would be a heavy load—and it wouldn't
even be enough for a whole day. But if they had
one more rat to help them, they could carry three
and three quarter pounds. The most logical choice
would be someone who worked with food, who
would be able to sneak it from the storeroom or
the kitchen without arousing suspicion. But when
Racso said her name out loud, Christopher recoiled.

"Isabella? I don't think she can keep a secret."

Racso shrugged. "What other choice do we have?"

"That's true. . . . If we could only make her feel she's a vital part of an important maneuver."

"I've got it!" Racso's eyes lit up. "We'll convince her to help us carry the food up there, and *then* we'll show her who it's for!"

"We'll have to show her from a distance," Christopher said nervously. "The big one doesn't know anything about us, and R-T has only met me. I don't want to upset him—he's been sick."

"Right, they said that on the radio—Nicodemus told us. He takes medicine every day for asthma. How much do you think he weighs?" Racso had taken a beaker of fluid down from the shelf.

"Gee, I don't know."

"We give this by weight." Racso measured out a large dose. "It's for rats with respiratory problems—in fact, you probably had it yourself when you fell out of the tree and punctured your lung. But we've made it even better since then." He put the beaker, almost empty, back on the shelf. "The effects should last for a couple of days." As he said these words Racso got a funny feeling, as if perhaps they had not thought clearly about exactly what they were doing.

"Christopher?"

"Yeah . . ."

"How *long* are we going to keep this a secret? I

mean, do you think they'll be around for more than a few days? I was just wondering, because of the medicine. . . ."

"I don't know," Christopher said. He didn't really want to think about that. "You leave that kind of stuff to me," he added.

Racso nodded. He was excited—very excited—to be in on the secret. He tried not to think about anything else.

There were problems with Isabella right from the start. For one thing, she couldn't get past the rule—which Nicodemus had told everyone the night before—that all the rats were supposed to stay inside for the next two days, in case a helicopter flew over.

"You tell me what it's about," she said. "Then I'll know whether it's worth breaking the rules for."

Christopher was all for dropping her right then, but Racso was patient.

"Isabella, you know we wouldn't ask you to help if there were anyone else who could do this, but there isn't."

"Well . . ." Isabella looked smug. "You're sure this isn't going to get me into trouble?"

"Of course not."

"Well . . . okay."

"What we have to do now"—Racso signaled for

Christopher to stay quiet, to let *him* handle it—"is to get about four pounds of food."

"Food! What kind of food?"

"A mixture—bread, nuts, carrots—stuff like that."

"I could get it from the kitchen, I guess. . . ." Isabella still looked doubtful. "We had acorns left over from supper last night."

"Acorns won't do," Christopher said quickly. "But walnuts would be fine . . . and peanut butter . . . maybe some raisins . . ."

"We're not stealing this stuff, are we?"

"Of course not." Racso sounded more certain than he felt.

Isabella just seemed to have trouble getting into the spirit of the adventure. She complained that her pack was killing her. Why had she let them persuade her to do this? She was sure she would get in trouble for it, just at the time she was trying to present a better image. Christopher was so disgusted with her that he couldn't even enjoy the thought of seeing R-T again. But there was no way out of it—they were almost to the cave. He ran ahead and scouted. There was no sign of the children.

"And how can you say it isn't stealing?" Isabella

went on. "You know the food belongs to the whole community, not just us."

"Be quiet!" Christopher ushered Racso and Isabella into the thicket. "You wait here. . . . I'm going into the cave to see if he's there."

"Who?" Isabella demanded. Racso signaled for her to hush. His eyes were bright with excitement.

Later Christopher wasn't sure why he hadn't thought about the other one being there. Maybe it was because R-T had been alone when he'd gone into the cave before. And when he first went in he didn't see her, only R-T, sitting cross-legged on the heap of pine needles he used for a bed. Christopher felt so happy to see him that he waved one paw and said cheerfully, "I told you I'd come back!" The little boy didn't smile. He looked scared. "I brought the food and medicine, just like I promised. . . . How are you feeling? My friend measured out a dose that should be perfect—"

That was when the stick came down. It hurt a lot, and it was so thick and thorny that it was just like being caught in a trap. Christopher yelped. He struggled to free himself, but the more he struggled, the more tangled up he got. His knapsack straps were stuck in some of the branches, and a thorn was piercing the tender flesh of his nose. R-T was just sitting there, not moving at all; but then she loomed over both of them, the end of the trap held firmly in both her hands.

"Let me go!" Christopher shrieked.

But she shook her head. Somehow she had managed to slip a string around his neck, and she was pulling on that, so that he was choking. She jerked the string with one hand and rammed him up against the wall of the cave with the branch, pushing the thick part hard against his chest.

"Give up!" she shouted.

Christopher struggled. He was aware of Racso and Isabella hiding outside, but he had no way to let them know he was in trouble.

"Give up!" she repeated. She rammed him harder with the stick. It hurt horribly. Christopher could hardly catch his breath to speak.

"Okay," he said. "I give up."

He was furious at her. The first thing she did was take another string—he noticed later that the laces were gone from her shoes—and tie it around all four of his paws. She drew the knot so tight that he couldn't move. Then she flipped him on his side and put the stick against his neck. She yanked the knapsack off his back. He could hear her rifling through the contents, pulling out the parcels, opening each one. After that she seemed to calm down a little.

He could hear R-T in the background, crying

softly. Once there was the sound of a struggle, and a thump, and louder crying. Eventually the girl picked up the string that bound him and carried him, head down, over to the door of the cave. She stared down at him with round, frightened eyes, the stick still in one hand. After the darkness, the bright sunlight made him blink. She continued to examine him, as if she couldn't believe her eyes.

"Who are you?" she said.

He spit some of the pine needles out of his mouth, trying to figure out what to do. She had already heard him speak, so there was no use pretending that he couldn't. He took a deep breath.

"I'm Christopher."

"Christopher who?"

"Just Christopher . . . that's my only name." He was afraid she would hit him again, but she didn't.

"Why can you talk?"

He tried to be careful. "My parents taught me."

"Animals don't talk." She sounded so angry and upset that Christopher knew answering would be pointless. She continued to stare at him miserably. If she hadn't hurt him so badly with the stick, Christopher could have felt sorry for her. He thought about R-T and the medicine and decided to try and reason with her.

"I'm a friend," he said quietly. "I brought food

[74]

for you this morning, and more when I came this afternoon. And I brought medicine for R-T."

"Why did you do everything in secret?"

"I was afraid of you."

She was quiet for a moment, realizing the truth of what he'd said.

"But you talked to Arthur."

"When he was sick. Somebody had to help him. I don't think it was very nice of you, leaving him alone the way you did."

Her eyes snapped. "I didn't really leave him. I was up on the ledge watching him the whole time. I just pretended to leave, to try to get him to tell me what he knew." Suddenly the anger left her, and her voice quavered. "I have to find a way to call my parents. We've been lost for three days. We've hardly even had anything to eat." The girl sat down and stared at him dolefully. She was still holding the string in one hand, but she had dropped the stick. Arthur came out and stood behind her. His lower lip stuck out. Christopher could tell he was unhappy.

"You should give him the medicine."

"Medicine!" The girl snorted. "You think I'm going to feed my brother rat medicine?"

"It will help him." Christopher tried to keep his voice level. "Our health practitioners make the potions from plants and minerals here in the valley."

"What do you mean, your health practitioners? You mean there's more than just you?"

"Uh . . ." Christopher could see now that he'd made a mistake. "A few more."

"Where are they?"

Two of them are in the thicket about twenty feet away from us, Christopher said to himself, but aloud, knowing that he was again being less than completely honest, he said, "They live in the valley."

"Down there?" She gestured down the slope.

He nodded.

"Are they all . . . like you?"

"What do you mean?"

It was her turn to hesitate. "Animals . . . rats?"

He nodded again.

"Do they have telephones?"

"No, no telephones. But they have food, and maps."

"A map wouldn't do us much good, not when there aren't any roads or towns or anything."

Christopher didn't say anything.

"Humph!" She strode away, her hands deep in her blue-jeans pockets. She appeared to be considering. After a while she came back. She picked up Christopher by the string, not nastily, but as if she had decided something.

"I want to get a message to your friends in the valley," she said. "I want them to lead me and Arthur out of here, back to where we came from. And I'm going to hold you hostage until they do that."

"Hostage?" Christopher frowned. "What's that?"

"Prisoner," said the girl. "And if they refuse to cooperate, I'll kill you."·

Christopher thought he was going to faint. He held his breath, then breathed deeply three times, fighting off dizziness. In the background—somewhere beyond the pounding of his own heart—he heard Arthur saying, "No! No! No!"

Chapter 9

Just like Arthur, she thought, to say his first word in two years in defense of a talking rat! She shoved more walnuts and a couple of raisins into her mouth, followed by a half slice of the bread. It tasted pretty good, she had to admit. But when she thought of who had made it, she shuddered. She was eating food that had been touched by rats! Yuck! She had to force the idea out of her mind. She thought again about Arthur. She had always known he could talk if he really wanted to. Wait until Leon heard about this!

She was weak. Ironically the food seemed to make her feel even weaker, but she knew it must be helping her. She had given half of it to Arthur. He gobbled it even though she'd told him to slow down. He wasn't as half starved as she was, though; he'd had most of the food from this morning, as well as the berries, and apparently the rat had left him some stuff the afternoon before.

The rat. It was lying on the floor of the cave, tied to a large rock. There could be no question about its talking. She had wondered, at first, whether it was stuffed and operated by remote control, with a tape inside it. But a tape couldn't answer questions the way it had. And it had bled when she tied it up. So it was alive. It reminded her of reruns of *The Twilight Zone* she'd watched on TV. I'm in the Twilight Zone, she thought. But it didn't seem funny.

She had given the medicine to Arthur. She'd found it in a small leather pouch in the knapsack, and had tasted it first herself: It was minty and slightly sweet, like honeysuckle. For some reason she trusted what the rat had said about it: that it wouldn't hurt Arthur. The rat seemed really concerned about Arthur! And Arthur liked it, too!

But what to do next? She had to get in touch with the rest of them, the ones that lived in the valley. If they could talk, could they also read?

"Hey, rat."

Christopher didn't move.

"Hey, rat . . . you . . . Christopher."

"What?"

"Can you read and write?"

"Of course I can."

"Well, pardon me. . . . You're probably a Harvard graduate." Margaret laughed uneasily. "What do you write on? Oh—I know—that paper you had the food wrapped up in. . . ." She retrieved it from a corner of the cave. "And to write with . . ." She thought out loud. "How about some blackberry ink? And I'd better take Artie while I go get it, since I can't trust him not to untie you while I'm gone." She took the boy by the hand and went out. She was back in minutes, some mashed-up berries in one hand, a broken twig in the other. She untied Christopher from the rock, leaving his paws bound, and lifted him unceremoniously by the shoestring. She took him to the doorway, where there was more light.

Her voice was brisk, businesslike. "I want you to write a letter."

The strength of Christopher's own voice surprised him. "I won't."

"What do you mean?"

"I mean I won't."

Margaret was surprised and puzzled. She hadn't expected the rat to resist, and she wasn't sure what to do. She decided to try another tack.

"Look," she said. Her voice was gentle, persuasive. "This is the best thing for you. The sooner you write the letter, the sooner your friends can help me. And the sooner you'll be free."

"I don't care."

"Why not?"

"Because you're mean. You were mean to R-T, and you were mean to me."

Margaret was exasperated. "Of course it *seems* like I'm mean—you're my hostage. I can't kidnap someone and then act like a creampuff, can I?"

Christopher didn't say anything. His jaw was set in a way that looked permanent.

"Look, you're not being realistic." Margaret took a deep breath. She couldn't believe she was defending herself to a rat. "I am *not* mean. Really."

Silence.

"Look, it's *survival*! I mean, how long do you think we could survive? We're *humans*, and we're not meant to live out here in the wilderness like you are. Don't you see?"

She looked for some sign of understanding on the rat's face, but his eyes were closed tight and he was completely still. It wasn't as if she could have a staring contest with him—if she'd been able to do that, she'd be pretty sure she could win, the way she usually did in the school cafeteria. The way he was acting made her nervous.

"All right," she said loudly. "I'm SORRY!"

The rat moved slightly and opened one eye.

"I'm sorry," she repeated. "I guess I hurt your feelings."

"You certainly did hurt my feelings!" Christopher swallowed. "It hasn't been any field trip for me, trying to help you two."

"You were really trying to help Artie, not me."

"Well . . ."

She saw the opening and took it. "Well, now you can really help him. You can write this letter to your friends."

"If I do, will you let me go?"

"Not immediately. . . ." She could see that the rat didn't completely understand this hostage idea. "See, I have to use you to get the others to cooperate. But I will free you eventually." She put the paper, berries, and twig down beside Christopher. "I'll tell you what to say."

"You'll have to untie my paw."

"I'll just loosen the string . . ."

Christopher dipped the "pen" into the middle of a ripe berry. "Go ahead."

" 'Dear Friends . . .' " Margaret watched with amazement as the rat produced a tiny, neat script. " 'I have been taken hostage'—that's h-o-s-t-a-g-e— 'by two children.' " She waited for Christopher to

[82]

catch up. " 'They are treating me well, but they will not let me go until someone helps them get home.' Now sign your name."

"You're not treating me well."

"Look, just sign your name, okay?"

Christopher's ears flattened in irritation, but he did sign his name. Margaret took the letter and inspected it. The rat had great penmanship! Her own handwriting was sprawling and large, so she printed in block letters below Christopher's message:

NOTIFY ME OF YOUR INTENTIONS WITH REGARD TO THE HOSTAGE WITHIN 24 HOURS.

Signed,

Margaret

"Where should I put it so that the others will find it?"

Christopher pretended to think hard about this. "Try putting it over by the stone, a little to the left of the thicket there."

"You really think they'll come so close? I thought you said they live in the valley."

"I think someone will find it," Christopher said. "If not, we can try another place tomorrow."

He slept badly. He was still tied up, and when he woke at dawn he was stiff and sore. He'd had bad dreams about the girl, who he now knew was called Margaret: dreams that he was being hurt trying to protect R-T. His real name, the girl had explained, was Arthur, but the family called him R-T, which she spelled A-r-t-i-e. She'd told him, whispering, that R-T was a "mental case" because he wouldn't talk or act his age. She knew that he could do better; but her parents ignored her opinion and let him get away with murder. Christopher was startled at that. He couldn't imagine the mild-mannered, gentle R-T hurting anyone. Oh no—she had laughed—that was only an expression, to get away with murder—it meant that the boy simply did whatever he wanted to, no matter what others expected of him. Christopher felt like saying, that sounds like you, not Artie; but he held his tongue.

Now he could hear the boy's quick, light breathing behind him, as mild in sleep as he was awake. In contrast Margaret's snoring was like the opening and closing of a creaky door. Then the boy stirred and sat up. Christopher felt a hand stroke his back.

Margaret woke up, groaning. She turned over, trying to go back to sleep, but eventually she gave up. She took Arthur by the hand and went outside. When they came back, there were blackberries for everyone, including Christopher; and there was something else, too: a letter.

Her hands shook as she opened it. The piece of

paper was larger, with the same slightly rough feel to it. The text was written in lavender ink, in a beautiful flowing script. She read it out loud.

My Dear Margaret,

The aforementioned rat, Christopher, has been placed in exile, and we do not wish that he be returned to us.

Thank you for providing a home for him, and best wishes for your continued stay at Thorn Valley.

Warmly,
Nicodemus

"WHAT!?" Margaret shrieked. She couldn't believe it. She stamped one foot, crumpled up the letter, screamed again, uncrumpled it, and looked at it to make sure she'd read it right. Arthur was so alarmed by her behavior that he jumped to his feet and stared.

Then Arthur's attention shifted. He had caught sight of Christopher. The little rat was lying curled up against the wall of the cave, sobbing his heart out.

"Try and pull yourself together," Margaret said. "Crying doesn't help."

There was no indication that her words were heard. She had been standing near the door of the cave for what seemed like hours, listening to the rat sob. For a while she'd thought he might be faking, that the whole thing had been some kind of setup that he was in on all along. But as time passed, and the crying continued, she came to doubt that. Not even she could have faked it for that long, and she'd done her fair share of faking. No, the rat was genuinely shook up.

And so, of course, was Arthur. Margaret watched as he tried to comfort the weeping animal. Then he sat down beside Christopher and began to cry himself. The tears rolled down his cheeks silently, and he sat with his arms dangling between his knees as if he were exhausted.

She read the letter again. "The rat has been placed in exile"—that meant they'd kicked him out, told him to get lost, which was more than likely what he was crying about. She wondered why they'd done it. Then the funny part: "Thank you for providing a good home. . . ." She scowled. To foist him off on her, in her situation, when they'd decided they didn't want him anymore! As if she could take care of someone else besides Arthur! Well, she wasn't going to put up with that, no way. But the problem was, she couldn't just dump him now, because Arthur had gotten attached to him. The whole thing was just infuriating! She jammed her fists into the pockets of her jeans and stepped out into the open, leaving the other two to cry.

She fetched more berries and another twig and sat down on the ground, turning the letter over so that a blank surface was facing her. She didn't bother to address the rat who had signed the message— she couldn't figure out his name anyway. Instead she just wrote, in large letters:

YOU MUST TAKE RAT BACK!
Signed,
Margaret.

She folded the paper, stuck it back over by the thicket, and set a rock on top of it so that it wouldn't blow away.

Chapter 10

The next morning Margaret deliberately stayed in the cave later than usual, giving them a chance to reply to her letter. She'd checked twice yesterday, but there was nothing. Nothing, that is, except that the rat had continued to cry for the rest of the day, despite her and Arthur's efforts to cheer him up. She'd tried to question him, to find out exactly why he was so upset, but every time she spoke to him, he burst into tears. She guessed he wasn't that thrilled with the idea of staying with her, either. She decided to check beside the thicket for a note.

The bright sun outside the cave made her half blind, and she stumbled to the thicket. *Her* note was gone, but there was nothing in its place. Disappointment fell like a blade across her chest. She sat down on the ground, her hands over her face.

"Pardon me."

She wasn't sure she had heard it, and she was afraid to look. A moment passed. Then it came again:

"Pardon me."

Margaret breathed deeply. She uncovered one eye. The sunlight made her blink; she uncovered the other one quickly. "Who is it?"

"It is I." The tone was formal. It took a minute for Margaret to see the rat who stood a bit in front of the thicket. He was gray and gnarled like the wood that grew on the side of the mountain, and in his front paw he carried a tiny gnarled stick: a cane. Margaret stared. The rat stood quietly, looking composed. Margaret opened her mouth, but nothing came out. She managed to squawk, "Who are you?"

"My name is Nicodemus."

"Nicodemus." She continued to stare at him. He *was* a rat, like Christopher, yet somehow he looked different. Clearly, he was older. Over one of his eyes was a dark patch, which, along with the cane, made him look sort of distinguished. But more striking was the way he stood so quietly, without fidgeting at all, looking straight at her.

"You're the one that signed the letter, aren't you?"

"Yes. And you must be Margaret."

Margaret was not sure what to say next. She had never thought a rat could be anything but a rat, which in itself was a disgusting thing to be; but this rat was different. He was cool and steady, and his gaze made her feel like looking away. Had she seen him before she'd sent the letters, she thought she would have asked directly for help, instead of mentioning the hostage. But it was too late now.

"Christopher's in the cave," she said.

"I supposed he would be."

"He's been crying and crying."

"Has he?"

"I think it was your letter that upset him," she said. "Where you said you didn't want him back."

"I see."

"And so I wrote you again, to see if you would take him."

"I got your letter." He had a small leather pouch across his chest, and he opened it and took out the crumpled piece of paper. "You must take rat back," he read aloud, with a quizzical expression. He looked up. "I couldn't understand it," he said. "I thought you wanted him."

"I did when I took him hostage, because I thought you wanted him, and if I kept him, then you'd help me. . . ." Margaret's voice had dropped.

"A rat who would steal food . . ." Nicodemus shook his head sadly.

"But he did that for *us*, really. I don't think it's fair to blame him for that."

"He could have asked."

"Maybe there wasn't time."

"Oh, there was."

She was silent, not knowing what to say next. Usually she found it easy to say *something*, no matter what the situation. Once she and Leon had been late to school for the umpteenth time, and she had to go tell the principal why. She'd made up a pretty good story. She wished Leon were here now. But instead there was just the little gray rat, staring at her with its one good eye.

"He likes my brother, Arthur," Margaret said. "He actually did it for him."

"How is your brother?"

"Oh, he's fine. To tell the truth, I've never seen him so good."

"That was a hard trip, over the mountain. I'm glad he's well." The rat smiled. He did seem glad. At the same time, Margaret thought the conversation was heading toward a close, and she knew she didn't want it to be over.

"Listen," she said. "What about Christopher?"

"What about him?"

"I can't keep him, actually. I've got enough problems of my own."

Nicodemus looked surprised. "Well, put him out."

"He might starve. You wouldn't want him to starve."

"Of course not."

"Listen, my brother and I need food, too. Until we find our way out of here." She kept her eyes glued to the ground. "I thought maybe you could help us. Christopher said there are a couple of you, and that you have supplies. I really hate to ask, but I don't know what else to do." She looked up at Nicodemus then, but he was tracing a line in the dust with his cane.

"We've worked for the food," he said quietly. "We couldn't just give it away."

"My parents could pay you later. They could send you a check."

"Hmmmmm . . . I'm afraid that wouldn't do. We don't use money."

"Maybe we could work for it, too, then. We're both bigger than you. I've done stuff like raking leaves and cutting the grass lots of times, for my dad," Margaret said, trying to keep the desperation out of her voice. She actually hated chores, and complained like crazy when she had to do them.

Nicodemus looked thoughtful. "There *is* a job we need done, but it's hard. It involves climbing a rather steep cliff. I'm not sure you could do that."

"I climbed this far, and I carried Arthur part of the way, too," Margaret pointed out.

"So you did." Nicodemus looked at her appraisingly. "You look strong."

Margaret blushed. Nobody had ever said that to her before. They'd used other words instead: words like stocky and fat.

Nicodemus continued. "There's a hawk's nest at the top of the cliff. We need to move it about a mile, to an oak tree in a meadow north of where we live. Once it's moved, the hawk will have a new hunting territory instead of the area around our nest." He drew a map in the dirt with his cane.

"You mean hawks eat. . . ?" Margaret was embarrassed to say the word "rats" to Nicodemus. It was as if saying it would acknowledge that he, too, was a rat; and he already seemed too wise for that.

But Nicodemus wasn't embarrassed at all. "*You* won't be in any danger from the hawk—that's why you could be such a help. She only attacks small mammals, birds, and fish. But the climb itself is dangerous. And if you succeed in reaching the nest, there may be other problems, too."

Margaret was surprised by her own honesty. "I don't know if I can do it or not, but I'll try."

"You're sure?"

She nodded.

"Then I'll send a guide to take you to the cliff—not today, but early tomorrow morning. She'll bring Arthur to our nest first, so he can be looked after.

Christopher can come with him. And we'll give you some food, too."

"Thanks."

"Good luck," he said. And he limped into the thicket without looking back.

Chapter 11

The guide was named Isabella. Margaret didn't like her right from the start. Following her through a meadow covered with flowers, Margaret pretended that she was alone. The flowers—purple, pink, and blue—were pretty, and she'd caught sight of a river flowing below a line of willow trees, off to the left. She hoped Arthur would be okay. She'd felt nervous leaving him, but Christopher had promised to look after him, and she was sure he would.

Isabella had brought food: dried fruit, nuts, juice, and bread—and a haughty explanation of Margaret's task. It was crucial that the hawk's nest remain intact, she had said, keeping her nose in the air as if something smelled bad. The homes of living creatures deserved respect. She'd glared at Margaret as if there was something else she wanted to say, but instead she'd taken off, without so much as a "follow me."

She never looked back to see if Margaret was still there. At the edge of the meadow the rat mounted a fallen tree and scampered across the trunk, jumping down into a hodgepodge of weeds and saplings. Margaret saw where she landed, but by the time she'd climbed up on the tree and begun inching her way across, Isabella was out of sight.

"Wait up!" Margaret shouted. She decided to try walking through the tall weeds under the tree trunk, to save time; but it turned out the ground there was marshy, and before she knew it, she was up to her ankles in water. She sloshed on. Finally the water stopped. She brushed aside saplings and brambles. In a small clearing beyond the brush sat Isabella, grinning broadly.

"You wait until I get my hands on you!" Margaret was so mad she thought she was going to pop.

Isabella laughed. "I didn't realize human children were so slow," she said.

"You just wait!" Margaret decided that she and the rat were going to have it out right there. She took a deep breath and marched across the clearing, but when she got within an arm's length of Isabella, the rat took off. "Better save your strength!" she

shouted over her shoulder. "You're going to need it!"

And so it went, Margaret whacking her way through the underbrush in the direction she thought the rat had turned, always on the verge of despair, encountering Isabella just when she'd grown certain she was completely lost. She decided she hated Isabella more than anyone in the entire world. She was just about to tell her so when she emerged from another thicket and found herself standing at the base of a cliff.

"That's it!" Isabella said triumphantly.

"That's what?"

"The nest!" Isabella smiled serenely and pointed straight up. Margaret stared. Far above her, sticking out from a little promontory of rock, was a mass of sticks and leaves. Just looking that high up made Margaret dizzy.

"You're kidding," she said.

Her voice must have been louder than she thought, because just after she spoke, she saw a dark shape rise from the promontory. The hawk hovered in the air, looking down. Then it made a screeching sound and flew away.

"You see?" Isabella said smugly.

"But how could anybody climb this? It goes straight up."

"It doesn't go *straight* up. Look. . . ." Isabella pointed to some places where the rock was cracked or indented. "You could use those to hold on to. And you have the vine rope we made for you."

"I don't think I can do it."

Isabella shrugged. "That's your decision."

Margaret despised the rat more than ever. She had known all along that it was impossible, had led Margaret to it knowing that it could not be done. She turned to Isabella. "I hate you," she said, "in case you're wondering."

"In case you were wondering, I hate you, too," Isabella said.

"Why?"

"Because you ruined my new image."

"I don't know what you're talking about!"

"Just when everyone had begun to accept that I'm really extremely responsible, not flighty or silly like they used to think, you came along. And I decided to help Christopher. So I climbed all the way up the mountain with the food I had taken out of the storeroom—*against* my better judgment. And what's the first thing that happens when we get there? You grab Christopher and tie him up! So we had to tell the whole thing to Nicodemus and Justin. Imagine how *I* felt!" Isabella's voice was low with fury. "And it was all your fault!"

[99]

"That's ridiculous! I didn't ask you to take the food out of the storeroom, or make you climb the mountain. I didn't know anything about you."

"But if you hadn't been there, it wouldn't have happened."

"Do you think I wanted to get lost in the middle of the wilderness? Do you think I want to be here now? Believe me, I'd ten times rather be home watching TV and drinking Pepsi! I don't like nature! And I don't like rats, either!" Margaret spat these words out. She thought this particular rat was the most horrible creature she'd ever met. She made Christopher look like an angel.

"It's your fault you kidnapped Christopher. And just when he was trying to help you, too!"

"Well . . ." Margaret felt confused about what to say. The rat had a point. But it was unfair to blame her for everything! "Maybe I'm not perfect," Margaret snarled. "Like you!"

Isabella sniffed, as if the argument were over and she had won. "And you'll never get that nest down, either. You're too fat to make it up the cliff."

Margaret felt herself swell with rage. She looked straight ahead and gritted her teeth to keep from screaming. She turned her back on Isabella, and then she just sort of threw herself at the rock, kicking, jabbing, clawing its surface. She stuck her knees into it and pushed up; she gouged it with her elbows;

she clenched it with all ten fingers. All the energy she had was gathered in her arms and legs, pushing upward. She was angry, angry, angry, and the madder she got, the higher she climbed. She didn't look down, and she didn't look all the way up, either. She was aware of the rat somewhere down below, watching her, but that wasn't important. There was only one thing that was important, and that was to get the nest. She would get it! She would!

But after a while she made a mistake, which was to check how much farther she had to go. She glanced up quickly. The point of rock on which the nest was perched was perhaps twenty feet above her, to her left. The thought came: I'm really high up! She began to tremble and sweat, and her breath came in short gasps. Her hands and feet felt cold and wet. She hugged the rock, resting her face against the cool dark stone. She could feel the sting of raw patches of skin on her wrists and elbows. She breathed deeply, leaning into the rock. There was nothing else to do but get the nest. She started up again.

Now she was careful as she climbed. She inched along each tiny ledge, making sure her hands had worked their way into some pocket of stone before she moved her legs. It was amazing, on a surface that seemed flat, that there were really so many hand- and footholds. In science class they had studied the making of rocks, and how certain kinds of stone had formed in the ages of the earth long before mammals. She was supposed to memorize the names of those ages, but she never had. So her test came back with a D, which meant she was supposed to take it home and get it signed. And she did take it home and get it signed—by Leon. His face had scrunched up with concentration as he copied her dad's signature off her old report card. The teacher hadn't known the difference. She didn't have to sign Leon's test, because Leon was a genius. He could learn things without bothering to study. He'd read hundreds of books, and he remembered everything.

She felt calmer, thinking about home. As she crept along the rock, she imagined her dad: If it were Saturday, he would be in his study, sitting in his lounge chair, a video playing on the TV. Sometimes he rented cartoons, and tried to get Margaret to watch them with him. He'd laugh at anything! She imagined his voice: "Easy does it, Margaret . . . you can do it. . . ." He wasn't a bad father, really, not as grown-ups went. Tears filled her eyes; she stopped, took another deep breath, and looked up. She was only five feet from the nest. Slowly, carefully, she crept up the rock. Her hand touched the ledge, was over the side of the ledge. There was a rib of stone that felt secure. She pulled, putting a bit of her weight against it, then more. It held. She grasped it with both hands and held on tight, kicking her way over the ledge. Her stomach was scraped, her knees were torn, but she'd made it! She lay quiet, exhausted.

After a bit she looked around. The nest was sitting on a shelf of rock almost fifteen feet across. It was strewn with bits of fur, feathers, and bone, garbage from the hawk's meals. She stood up shakily. At the back of the shelf the cliff rose still higher—another fifty feet, at least. She reached into her pocket and dug out some raisins. For some reason they tasted like the most wonderful food she'd ever had. She thought of Isabella, waiting for her down at the bottom. Oddly, she didn't even feel that mad at her anymore! She called down, "I made it!"

There was a silence, then Isabella's voice, "You *did?*"

"Yep, I'm up here with the nest!"

"Oh!" Then a pause; then, a bit grudgingly, but only a bit, "That's GOOD!"

She set to work. She passed the vine rope under the bottom of the nest, as if she were putting ribbon on a birthday present, then tied a knot about four inches up. She would lower it down the side of the cliff as if it were a basket, wait for Isabella to untie it, then pull the rope back up to use for her own descent. She did this quite successfully, although the nest got caught on several outcroppings of rock on the way down, so that she had to jerk the rope to free it. But eventually Isabella called, "I've got it." Margaret pulled the rope up hand over hand. She tied a loop of it around the base of a boulder and secured the other end around her waist. She would lower herself down gradually, using the line as a brake.

But it didn't work exactly as it was supposed to. As she lowered herself over the side Margaret realized that she would have only the strength of her hands and arms to support her until she could rest her weight somewhere. She was dangling in midair! The side of the cliff was about four feet away, too far to reach. She kept her hands in close to her chest and grasped the lower part of the rope between her knees. She wormed her way down, bit by bit. Eventually she came to a spot where she could stick out her foot and touch the rock. A bit farther down she saw a tiny knob of stone she thought she could stand on, if she could just get over to it. She ignored the aching in her arms and kicked the rock in front of her, pushing herself out from the cliff. When she swung back she reached for the knob with both feet, but missed. She tried again, this time swinging out even farther, swinging back, grasping—got it! She leaned her knees and shoulders into the rock and stood resting precariously on the knob. Her arms hurt badly, and her palms were scraped and bruised. But she had done something remarkable, amazing, the kind of thing most people saw only on television! She, Margaret, had performed an extremely dangerous mission. There was no question that this was the greatest thing she had ever done! She rested her head against the rock.

She wasn't sure whether the sound was something she heard or just thought she heard: a whirring somewhere far off in the distance, a buzzing similar to a bumblebee's, but too slow, too regular. It seemed to come from the other side of the cliff, beyond the mountain. Helicopter! She gasped. Her mouth formed the word No! and she shrank into the rock. But that's crazy, she thought. I WANT to be found. I *do* want to be found, of course I do. She listened, but the noise was gone.

Chapter 12

"How was I supposed to know it was part of the plan?" Christopher's voice was strained. "I thought you meant it!"

Nicodemus was gentle. "Do you really think we'd put you into exile?"

"I didn't know. But I did know I should have told you about them."

"Yes, you should have."

"I wanted the secret for myself. And I knew you'd say not to go near them anymore."

"That's probably true."

"Arthur needed me. He was sick and half starved."

"Yes." Nicodemus looked at Christopher attentively, then shifted slightly in his chair. They were in his office, a small room with a wooden desk, chairs, and bookcase. "Having the children here presents difficulties," he said. "There's a lot they don't know, but what they've seen and heard is dangerous for us. It would have better been avoided."

"You're angry."

"No." The old rat shook his head. His voice was stern, but he looked at Christopher fondly. "It's just that I haven't been feeling well, and the trip up and down the mountain was tiring."

"I'm never tired," Christopher said. "Only hungry."

"Yes," said Nicodemus, smiling. "I've noticed." And he dismissed Christopher with a wave of his paw.

Racso had agreed to baby-sit Arthur while Christopher was talking with Nicodemus. In fact he had looked forward to the opportunity. There were many things about city life that he missed, and he was hoping Arthur could give him an update. The boy was sitting cross-legged by the creek, eating raisins one by one. Racso sat on his haunches in front of him.

"I was just wondering how things are going in the candy industry," he said brightly. "Candy is my favorite food, and we don't get much of it here."

Arthur was pleased but confused. He liked candy, too. His mother had been in the habit of buying him a candy bar every time she went to the grocery store. He could picture the wrapper clearly in his mind. He licked his lips and looked at Racso. But Racso didn't give him any candy. He just kept talking.

"One of my favorites is the Peppermint Pattie," he told Arthur confidingly. "When I had a chance, I always got that first, especially if it was a hot day. I think peppermint tastes so good on a hot day. And when I came to Thorn Valley—that's here, you know, that's what it's called here—I discovered they didn't have any candy. I really felt sorry for them. So I worked and worked, and I made them a whole bunch for a surprise! To be honest with you, Isabella helped, too. Christopher was real sick then, but we snuck in and gave him some anyway. And he loved it! It helped him get well. And everyone else loved it, too." Racso sighed. "It's mostly gone now. I've been wanting to make some more, but I've just been so busy!"

Arthur kept thinking that Racso was going to give him some candy, even though Racso hadn't said so. He checked to see if Racso had pockets where a candy bar might be hidden, but he didn't. He wondered if Racso had any money. To get candy you had to have money. But Racso didn't have pockets to put the money in.

"What's your favorite kind of candy?" Racso asked.

Arthur didn't answer.

"Don't be shy," Racso said. "You don't have to be shy with me. I know what humans are like—I come from the city myself. Some of these other rats don't know about the kind of stuff that you and I know about, because they've always lived here in the valley. They live the natural way—no TV, no comics. I like it here now, but it does take some getting used to. Sometimes I sit and remember this store I used to sneak into at night. It was just one room, and across the front there was a great big counter, and along the counter there was every kind of candy bar in the whole world. And they were lined up according to color. First there were the Hershey bars, which are brown, then next to them were the plain M&M's, and next to them were the Tootsie Rolls, then the reds: Mounds bars, Kit-Kat—I didn't like Kit-Kat, because it had the word "cat" in it, so I wouldn't eat that. Anyway, there were Nestlé's Crunch and Almond Joy, 'cause they're blue, you know, and . . ."

Suddenly Racso realized that Arthur was crying. He'd been so carried away by his memories that he'd almost forgotten about the boy. "What's wrong? What's the matter?" he asked.

Arthur opened his mouth and moaned. He wanted candy. In his mind he thought the words: want candy. He opened his mouth and moaned again.

[109]

Wouldn't you know that Christopher would arrive right then? Racso was mortified.

"What have you done to him?" Christopher shouted. "He's crying!"

"I *know* he's crying!"

"You were supposed to be taking *care* of him!"

"I *was* taking care of him!" Racso was exasperated. "I was just talking to him about some things we have in common. And when I looked up—"

"When you looked up! You shouldn't have looked away in the first place!"

"Pardon me," Racso said, "but look at him right now."

Arthur had stopped crying and was smiling instead: smiling at the antics of Seymour and Michaelina, who were wrestling with each other in a puddle of dust. Their tails whipped back and forth and they tumbled over and over, screeching, *"EEEEE! EEEE! EEEE!"*

Arthur laughed out loud. He had forgotten about the candy.

"Hmmmm," Christopher said. "I guess he's okay after all."

"Guess so."

"I'm going to take him for a walk. Want to come?"

"No, thanks."

Racso went back to the laboratory, still dreaming

about the candy bars, while Christopher and Arthur strolled up the walk from the pine grove to the back door of the nest.

Christopher brought the things he wanted to show Arthur outside, one by one.

"This is my bowl—see how it's got my name carved on it? And this is the journal I keep for school. I write down my ideas in here, and all the exciting things that happen—I wrote about you, too. And this is a jar of pokeberry ink. We use it to write with. Never drink this—it's poisonous! Last year I wanted to see how poisonous it was, so I mixed some with water and drank just a little bit. Was I sick!" Christopher laughed.

"And this is a game you play with sticks and balls. See, you hold this stick with your tail—if you have one, that is—and you whack the ball into the basket." Christopher demonstrated how this was done. He chased the ball around in circles until he was panting, then went over to the bamboo faucet near the nest and turned it on to get a drink. Arthur got down on his knees and got a drink, too. He liked the little piece of wood that switched the faucet on and off.

"Now we'll go for a walk," Christopher said.

They strolled beside the stream. Christopher chatted happily, telling Arthur about how he'd met Racso and how they became friends. "We got assigned to work in the garden together while some of the other rats were away. Neither of us would admit we couldn't read the list of instructions, so we ended up picking all the mint instead of weeding it. But that wasn't the first time I'd gotten into trouble—not at all.

"When I was really little, and used to eat in the nursery, they always brought in soup first, then bread. One day I decided to have my bread first. By the time I got to the soup, it was cold. So I found there *was* a good reason to eat the soup first. But I had to figure it out for myself.

"That's how I am about everything. I'm always trying new things, like walking backward instead of headfirst, and sleeping in the daytime but staying up all night. 'Just do what I tell you,' my dad says, and my mom says, 'Christopher, why can't you trust our experience?' But it isn't that I don't trust them, Artie—I just like to see for myself.

"There are lots of ways to do things—I learned that from Racso. He came here from the city, like you, and he had been brought up differently. He taught me about rock-and-roll music and tall buildings and cars and junk food and TV. In school I learned that the earth is covered with many cities and countries and they all have different ways of doing things.

"That's why I get impatient, doing the chores the same way each time. Nicodemus says I have to do them anyway. He says I have to figure out a way to keep from getting bored so quick.

"But I could never be bored around you, Artie. Everything about you is interesting. Someday you'll tell me all about yourself—about your mom and dad and what your house is like, and what you like to play with . . . one day, when you feel like it."

Arthur wished he *could* tell Christopher about his home. But as usual the words stuck in his throat. His bowl didn't have his name on it, like Christopher's, but it did have a picture of a dump truck in the middle. If you finished your cereal you could see it. And he had games, too, just like Christopher: a box where you stuck different shapes in different holes, and a clown that popped back up when you knocked him over.

"You haven't gotten sick since that day by the cave," Christopher said gently.

That was true. Arthur had drunk a dose of the medicine this morning, though; and Racso thought he should have two more doses, whether he got sick or not. This medicine was special because Racso had helped invent it. It came from plants that grew by the pond and in a special part of the garden; they had been ground up and mixed together. Racso

[113]

said when you drank it, part of the valley went inside you. Arthur had had lots of medicines before: pills and shots and sprays and spoonfuls of gooky stuff. But none of the doctors had been like Racso. You could pat Racso.

Christopher went down a bank to a sand beach beside the creek and drank. He splashed water with his tail. Arthur sat down and pulled his sneakers off. The water felt nice. He saw his reflection: His face looked bigger than he remembered, and it was smiling. He knocked a hole in it, laughing. Christopher laughed, too. Arthur waded into the stream. He squatted down and let the water run through the seat of his pants, and splashed his chest. He was taking a bath! But there was no soap! He laughed again.

Later they lay on the beach and let the sun dry them. Arthur fell asleep on the warm sand. When he woke up there were blackberries and bread to eat. The warm breeze carried the scent of honeysuckle and wild roses.

"There's just one more thing I want to show you," Christopher said on the way home. He took Arthur to a knoll where an oak tree grew. Pulling back the vines at the base of the trunk, he showed him how the soft ground underneath formed a hollow spot like a pocket.

"This is a secret place," Christopher explained. "I found it when I was little. I've never told anyone else about it—not till now. It's going to be for us." He paused to let the effect of this sink in.

"I might leave a present here for you, or a message, or something special to eat; and you might leave something here for me. But we won't tell anyone. That's what secret means, you know."

Arthur nodded.

"And we'll pledge to keep it a secret, because we're such good friends. They do that in stories. Let's see, the pledge will go like this. . . ."

Christopher talked for a while about the "Brother-hood of Rat and Child," using phrases like "by my troth and sacred honor" and "heretofor, theretofor, and in eternity." Arthur couldn't understand what he was saying, but he knew he could keep a secret. After all, he'd kept a secret from his parents and Margaret. It was in his closet.

"And we do swear . . ." Christopher said. "Put your hand here, Artie, and I'll raise my paw . . . that's right." The rat made sure they were just touching. "And we do thusly swear," he ended solemnly. "Our pledge shall live forever and our friendship abide, into eternity."

Chapter 13

Isabella wasn't exactly ashamed of the way she'd treated Margaret, but she had a feeling it wasn't going to sound good after what the girl had accomplished. So when she saw Margaret coming down the cliff, holding on to the rope and balancing against the rock wall with her feet, Isabella decided to be civil. She found this manageable if she didn't look right *at* Margaret. For example, she said, "Congratulations," while staring at the top of a long-needled fir tree, and "I didn't think you could do it," with her eyes fixed on her own toenails. Then she glanced at Margaret out of the corner of one eye.

"You're bleeding!" she screamed. "Oh my gosh you're BLEEDING! *THAT'S BLOOD!*"

"Of course it's blood," Margaret said. "I scraped myself on the rocks."

"But you need bandages! Medicine! First aid! HELP!" Isabella had never been good at dealing with injuries. If she cut herself in the kitchen, she always sent for Racso to put on the Band-Aid. Looking at the blood was just too upsetting. But Racso wasn't here now.

Margaret rolled up the legs of her jeans. Her knees were raw. When she bent them, blood trickled down her calves. She gulped. She felt like she was going to throw up, and then, suddenly, she did. Isabella screamed and closed her eyes. "Help, Racso!" she begged. But there was no reply.

She wasn't sure later what made her think of the new image: the Isabella who was steady, strong, and resourceful. But gradually she managed to calm herself. She took deep breaths and thought, What would Nicodemus do now? Justin? Beatrice? Elvira? And suddenly she knew! She remembered a day when they'd been on a picnic, and a baby rat had cut his leg on a sharp stone. Elvira had directed the others to pick comfrey along the banks of the creek. They had dipped it in the water and made a poultice, wrapping strands of the herb around the wound. And she could recognize comfrey, because they sometimes put it in the salad at dinner.

"Wait right here!" she shouted at Margaret. "I know what to do! Just lie down and wait for me!" And Isabella raced off toward the stream.

Later Margaret had to agree that it really helped. The cool green stuff reminded her of seaweed. The scrapes on her elbows, wrists, and knees stopped burning, so that before long she could walk without wincing. Isabella was different this time: slow, considerate, stopping often to explain where they were. Carrying the nest was awkward, but it did fit in a forked branch in the oak tree. The walk back was like a dream for Margaret; she had never been so tired in her life, and as soon as she got to the glade where she'd left Arthur and Christopher, she lay down on the moss by the stream and fell asleep.

"She moved the nest!" This cry entered Margaret's dream and repeated itself over and over. The voice that uttered it was high and shrill: Isabella's? But the repetition was odd, as if there were a hundred rats echoing the news. Margaret was dimly aware of someone replacing the poultices on her arms and legs, but the voice that accompanied the soothing sensation seemed to be one she hadn't heard before. She was aware of a background hubbub, like static on the telephone. And she felt she could sense the presence of many small bodies around her. She reached out once in her sleep, to see if she could touch them, but there was nothing there. By the time she awoke there was only Arthur, sitting cross-legged on the ground, with Christopher beside him.

"We heard you moved the hawk's nest," Christopher said. He felt as if he should thank Margaret, but he couldn't bring himself to.

She nodded. "It was scary, but I liked it."

"Why?"

"Nobody ever asked me to do anything that important or that hard." She looked at Christopher awkwardly. "I'm sorry about what happened in the cave. I was afraid, and I didn't know what to do."

"I guess it wasn't that bad an idea, from your point of view," Christopher said ruefully. He rubbed the sore spot on his nose. "Anyway, it worked out all right."

She nodded. "You know, I think I like it here," she said softly. She looked at her little brother. "I think Artie does too."

"But she likes it here," Christopher said. "She told me she did." He was standing in Nicodemus's office with Racso and Justin. Nicodemus was sitting at his desk. "And furthermore, she can keep on helping us, like she did with the hawk's nest. Think how fast she could move that pile of stones down by the dam."

"But then she would know about the dam."

"What does it matter if she knows? She knows a lot already."

"What do you mean?"

"She knows we can talk and read and write." Justin shot a significant glance at Christopher, who winced. "Will it really make any difference if she learns there are more of us than she thought?"

"I see what you mean," Nicodemus said slowly. "It wouldn't make her story any more believable. As long as they don't know about NIMH, that is."

"What story?" Christopher asked.

"The one she tells when she gets back where she came from."

"Oh, she can't go back. That would be crazy."

"Did you think she and Arthur would stay here forever?" Nicodemus asked Christopher.

Christopher hadn't really thought about that. He didn't know what to say.

"I don't think they'd be happy here," Nicodemus said softly. "They'd miss their parents and friends."

"They're happy now," Christopher argued. "Artie hasn't been sick at all. And he needs me. I'm his best friend."

"Having a special friend makes you feel special, too, I bet."

Christopher's throat tightened. Everybody else had someone: Racso had Isabella, and Justin had

Beatrice . . . "Arthur *needs* me," he repeated. "He can't talk, but I can understand him by the way he looks at me."

"I'm glad it was you who found him," Nicodemus said.

Christopher brightened. "He can stay, can't he?"

"I don't know what's going to happen. But for now, I think you should look after him. Make sure he's comfortable and that he has whatever he needs to eat or play with."

"I will," Christopher smiled widely. "Oh, I will."

Normally Margaret didn't like parties, but when Christopher said this one was in her honor, she could hardly refuse to come. And he'd said something about more rats, too.

But this! During the evening Margaret tried to count them, but they came and went so quickly that she couldn't get an accurate number. Racso and Christopher were there, of course, and Isabella and Nicodemus, too. But besides them there were others, light and dark, big and small, shy and friendly.

She couldn't keep from enjoying herself. There was music, and everyone sang "Froggie Went a 'Courting" and "Old McDonald Had a Farm." Then Racso climbed up on a stump and crooned, "Climb Every Mountain," which he dedicated to Margaret

[121]

and Isabella. He also sang "Love Me Tender" and "You Ain't Nothin' but a Hound Dog," which all the rats seemed to like. Many of them danced, swaying on their haunches and swinging their tails back and forth. Margaret felt funny, being so big, but to her astonishment Arthur jumped up and danced, too. He pumped his arms back and forth and let his head roll across his shoulders, and at the end of each song he spun around in circles until he fell down. Then he crawled over and helped himself to the wooden trays loaded with raisin cookies and peaches and nuts and grape juice and raspberry tarts. Margaret loved the tarts, too. She ate a whole trayful, popping them into her mouth two at a time. Then she looked down, and Nicodemus was at her side.

"Congratulations. And thank you."

"Oh." Margaret felt embarrassed. "Maybe I should thank you," she said weakly. "I never would have done it if you hadn't made me."

"I made you try, but you succeeded all on your own. And it was a very hard task."

"You thought I could do it all along, didn't you?" She stared at the old rat sitting so peacefully beside her. How had he known that about her?

"Yes, I did." He met her gaze gravely. "I thought you could do it because you'd already done such wonderful things."

She couldn't believe her ears. Was he talking about her, Margaret? "What do you mean?" she asked.

"You saved your brother's life—you found him food and shelter. And you captured Christopher and figured out a plan to get you and Arthur back home."

"You mean holding him hostage?"

He nodded, then smiled. "I'm not suggesting that I approve of the plan, but under the circumstances it was resourceful."

"I wouldn't have hurt him, really."

Margaret would have liked to say that she wasn't really wonderful at all. Suddenly she remembered the morning in the principal's office when she and Leon had been late, and she'd made up the story about how an old lady in a blue Buick had tried to kidnap them. The principal hadn't really believed her, but he'd let them into class without a note, and that was all she'd cared about, anyway. She wouldn't have told that lie to Nicodemus.

Nicodemus got to his feet. "I've got to go—I told Beatrice I'd dance with her. I'll see you later."

"Okay."

Margaret watched the dancing, letting her head sway with the rhythms of the music. She felt full inside, but the fullness wasn't just food. What is it? she asked herself. And the answer came back: I'm happy.

After that she did dance, first with Racso, then with Isabella, and finally with Christopher. She showed them the break-dancing steps Leon had taught her; when she got down on the ground, Christopher jumped on her back and started dancing on top of her, spinning and whirling while she did the same thing underneath him. Racso tried it then, but he ended up flipped on his back with all four legs treading the air at once.

"Like this." Margaret showed him how she used her forearms to pivot on. She felt great. She wasn't a good break-dancer, but nobody knew the difference. They called out, "Go . . . Go . . . Go," and she danced faster and better than she ever had.

After a while Arthur got tired of dancing. He watched Margaret for a few minutes, but then he wandered away. The air was full of lightning bugs, and a big orange moon hung over the side of the mountain.

He decided to take a walk. He walked until he came to the secret place. The branches of the great oak formed a roof under the sky. For a while he sat underneath the tree, leaning his small back against its trunk. He said aloud the word he had spoken when he thought Margaret was going to hurt Christopher. He said it loud, then softly, then as a question: No? The spoken words seemed like bubbles: delicate, magical, floating in the air until they finally sailed away.

He got up and pulled away the vines as Christopher had shown him. He bent close to the smooth hollow and found a feather there, a present from his friend. He rubbed the soft edge against his cheek. He decided to carry it with him on his walk.

After a time he came to the bamboo faucet where Christopher had gotten a drink. He pulled the little piece of wood up. The water came on. He drank, and then took off his shoes and wet his feet. He could hear the music coming from the clearing near the stream. He danced for a while. The ground under the faucet turned sticky with mud. He stuck his feet in the warm, oozy mud. The water formed a little river, rolling down toward the hole where Christopher had come and gone, bringing the bowl, the journal, the game. Arthur put his arm in the hole. He felt smooth, cool earth, nothing more. He went back to the mud and picked some up in his hands. You could mold it into shapes, like Play-Doh. He touched it to his lips, then spit it out. There was more and more mud, and when he jumped in the mud, water splashed everywhere.

Chapter 14

Justin didn't go to the party. He had a headache, probably from trying to figure out how to handle the situation with the human children. He went to bed early, nestling into his mattress of dried grass, and was instantly asleep.

He woke up under strange circumstances. It was not morning, he was sure of that; the sky was still dark through the window, and far off he could hear strains of music: the party. He glanced around the room; everything was in its place. He closed his eyes again, almost drifted off, and then opened them. There was a strange smell in the air: a dank, wet smell.

He opened his door and then slammed it shut, staring at a stream of water spreading across the floor. He grabbed a bit of wood and flung the door open again. The water in the hall was at least four inches deep! Holding the wood in one forepaw to help him float, he half scrambled, half swam for the main door. The current was with him. That meant the flood must be coming from the rear entrance. He breathed deep, swam harder. The water picked him up and deposited him with a *splosh!* on the ground outside. Should he run for help, or check the source? On a hunch he ran around to the rear. A muddy pond was draining into the open door of the nest, and the faucet was still running. The human child, covered in mud, lay sound asleep on the clay rise just above the door. "Turn off the faucet!" Justin yelled. The child didn't stir. Justin plunged into the pond, keeping his head above the swill. He reached the water pipe and turned it off with his teeth.

"What do you mean, it didn't do that much damage?" Justin glared at Christopher. "It could have collapsed the lower section of the nest! If I hadn't stayed home from the party, we could have lost everything!"

"Not only that, but all the flour in the storeroom was turned to paste." Isabella was distraught. "We were saving it for winter. I don't know what we'll do now."

"There's time to harvest more," Beatrice said. "And we can always make acorn flour."

"He didn't know what he was doing," Christopher said. "It's not fair to blame him."

"I'm not blaming him," said Justin. "I'm blaming *you*. I thought you'd agreed to keep an eye on him. You let him wander away, and look what happened."

"Maybe we could put a collar on him," Racso suggested. "Humans do that for dogs and cats, you know."

"Shut up! He's not a pet!"

"I was just trying to help!"

"You were not. You were trying—"

Nicodemus interrupted. "The truth is, this isn't a good place for a human child. The boy will have to be watched carefully, so he doesn't do more damage." He turned abruptly and went back to his office.

Margaret felt bad about the flood. She tried to make up for it by working extra hard. She helped the rats build their new dam, moving a great pile of stones and then placing them one by one in the clay mortar. She dug trenches for the irrigation system with a wooden spade carved especially for her. She learned to recognize most of the rats by name: Racso, Justin, Beatrice, Brendan, Sally, Brutus,

Nolan, Mitchell, Fern. They seemed like friends now. At the end of a long day it was hard to remember everything they'd talked about: There were jokes and teasing, chatter about the progress of the work, how hot it was, what Isabella was cooking for dinner. Out of habit the rats scanned the sky for the hawk, but it didn't reappear. Margaret learned more about them. But when she asked where they'd come from and how they'd ended up in the valley, they changed the subject or pretended they hadn't heard.

Sometimes Margaret got angry. The work was hard; her fingernails broke, and her hands were covered with small cuts. Racso gave her medicine to rub on the raw places. Still, some days she felt like a slave. "You can't make me work," she'd shout at the others. "I can do whatever I want to! I don't have to help you!"

"I didn't say you did," someone responded.

Margaret stalked away and sat by herself under a pine tree. Still, when supper was dished up that evening, she felt a little funny about asking for seconds. And the next day she went back to work.

She lost count of the days. Her sweatshirt grew grimy and ragged; she tried washing it, but without soap the water didn't make much difference. The reflection of her face in the pond looked thinner, and the waistband of her jeans got so loose that she had to hold it up with a belt made of vines.

Sometimes the rats' food was good; other times, awful. The worst was a paste of acorns, carrots, and onions. She'd seen fish in the pond, and had asked the rats about fishing, but Isabella explained that they didn't kill animals for food, especially since there was plenty to eat otherwise. So acorns it was.

With the help of the rats Margaret built a hut out of saplings for her and Arthur to sleep in. It was a round house, like a bubble, at the base of a large straight pine. She wove leafy vines through the saplings to make the walls and roof. Isabella showed her how to braid wild grasses from the meadow, and these they tied over the vines on the top to keep out the rain. The floor was thick and soft from layers of pine needles. Margaret and Arthur slept in the hut every night. In the morning she waited for Christopher to come play with Arthur before she left for the day's work.

She thought about home. The funny thing was that it seemed like a dream now, the fact that all her life she had lived in a brick house and slept in a bed with sheets, eaten her food off a china plate, worn clean clothes, spent the evenings eating candy or potato chips and watching TV. She thought about how different it was back there when she got a drink of water: how she'd look in the cupboard or the dishwasher for a clean glass, turn on the faucet, watch the water flow out from the pipes that ran under the streets of the city. Then she'd put the dirty glass in the sink. Now when she was thirsty she would walk down to the stream, cup some water into her hand, and drink it. It wasn't that one way was better or worse, but they were so different.

There were some things at home that *were* better, though. One was mosquito repellent. Racso had tried to develop some for her, but most mornings both she and Arthur crawled out of the hut covered with pink-and-white bumps. She gave up trying not to scratch them. The next day's would itch worse, and then she would scratch *them*, and the old ones would disappear.

She still talked to Leon in her mind. She wondered if he'd gotten the skateboard he wanted for his birthday. She wondered if he thought about her. He would miss her, she guessed. She wondered whether he'd been able to save fifty dollars to buy a scooter— he'd bet her that he'd have all the money by the end of the summer. Now she didn't know when that was. In her mind she asked him if he'd saved any, but it was like talking to a ghost.

She tried not to think about her parents. When she imagined their faces, looking happy or sad or thoughtful, she got an awful feeling inside, sort of like sickness, but heavier and sadder. She remembered how her dad had forced her to go on the camping trip, so she'd have a chance to be outdoors and away from the city. She'd resented it, of course. But when she smelled the wildflowers in the meadow, or walked under the starry sky, she wished he could be with her. How he would have loved the valley! But he was far away; he didn't even know where she was, or that she'd changed.

She missed her mother, too. She could picture her pale face and carefully set blond hair perfectly. The image would come to mind when she was least expecting it: at dinner with the rats, or walking in the woods at night. When it came she would feel like crying out, as if someone had hit her. That was strange, because back in the city, if there had been anyone from whom Margaret wanted to escape, it was her mother. Her mom had spent so much time trying to change the way she dressed, the way she spoke, the way she acted. "Just leave me alone!" Margaret used to shout, and then she'd slam the door to her bedroom as hard as she could.

But there were other things about her mom Margaret couldn't forget. Like the time her mom had spent all day trying to find just exactly the kind of Day-Glo wallpaper Margaret wanted for her bedroom, and had found it, and been almost as pleased as Margaret herself. Like the time she'd had Margaret's birthday party at the mall, and let all the kids have as many hamburgers and shakes as they wanted.

Like the time Margaret and Leon were the only kids who weren't invited to Elinor Huber's party, and her mom had taken them to hear the Purple Maniacs instead.

Margaret wondered what she was doing right now. Maybe she was in the kitchen, listening to classical music on the radio, her hands deep in a ball of bread dough. Maybe she was sketching: Her drawings of Margaret and Artie were hanging in the living room. They were good, too! But probably she was worrying: worrying about the kids. She'd always worried some, but this was probably the worst thing that had ever happened to her! Margaret wished there was a way to let her know that they were okay. Once, when she'd been alone, she'd even shouted, "We're all right!" just as loud as she could, over and over. But the words echoed back from the mountainside.

She talked about home with the rats, too. Christopher, especially, was curious, but all the rats liked to hear stories about Margaret's life.

"What do you do when school is out?" someone asked. "Do you play all day?"

"I have to set the table and take out the trash, but after that, I can do whatever I want. Usually Leon and I do stuff together. Most days in the summer we take the bus downtown to his grandmother's house. She's this little black lady, about a million years old, and she lets us do things our parents would kill us for."

"Like what?"

"Like eat a gallon of ice cream all at once, or dress up in the old clothes in her attic and wear them in the high rise next door. Her attic is full of neat stuff: old science magazines, and an old microscope, and a wind-up phonograph. She's got six cats, too, and a chihuahua."

"What's a chihuahua?"

"It's a little dog, not much bigger than you. He's named Pedro." Margaret laughed out loud, remembering their adventures. "Once we crawled up on the roof and made a whole bunch of paper airplanes. We wrote crazy notes in them and threw them down at people who were walking by."

"Did you get into trouble?"

Margaret shook her head. "Somebody did go and complain. But you know what Leon's gram said? She said, 'I'm too old to worry about stuffed-up people like you. You ought to learn how to laugh, then you wouldn't have to come banging on an old woman's door!'" Margaret talked in a high voice. "Then she called, 'You children come and have some cake!'"

"What kind of cake?" Racso's mouth watered.

"Coconut. That's Leon's favorite."

"Do coconuts grow here, in the valley?" Little

Michaelina looked as if she were about to run into the woods to try and find one. Margaret and Racso laughed.

"They grow in Hawaii," Margaret explained. "They're big and white and waxy, not like walnuts or hazelnuts."

"And they use them in candy, like Mounds bars." Racso was proud of his special knowledge. "They're delicious."

"I want to go to the city," Michaelina whined. "Thorn Valley is no fun!"

"I love the valley!" Margaret didn't plan the words; they just popped out. The scent of pine wafted from the fir trees overhead.

"You do?" Michaelina looked surprised.

Margaret nodded, but *she* was surprised, too. She hadn't known she loved anything.

Chapter 15

Arthur was doing well. He had drunk two more doses of Racso's medicine, and his breathing seemed normal, even at night. His skin had turned tan, and his hair was bleached by the sun. On his side of the hut he kept a collection of gifts Christopher had given him: a feather, some pretty stones, a little pocketbook made of braided reeds, a whistle. He lined these up in a row every morning, and if Margaret tried to touch one, he shrieked. Once she even heard him say the word "Mine."

"I always knew you could talk, Artie. I knew you were just faking."

He stuck out his tongue.

"You'll be sorry." Margaret scowled. "One of these days you'll need my help. And when it happens, I'll remember the day you stuck your tongue out at me and think: No way!"

Arthur laughed. He knew Margaret was just scolding. Anyway, if he needed help, all he had to do was find Christopher.

He and Christopher were together all day long. They ate breakfast on the flat rock near the entrance to the nest: fruit and raisin bread and dry cereal that tasted sort of like cornflakes. Then they went for a walk. Sometimes they followed the stream that crisscrossed the meadow, and sometimes they climbed partway up the mountainside, following one trail, then another. Christopher had started a club called the Brave Explorers. He and Artie were the only members.

Arthur liked Christopher a lot. He liked to pick him up and pat his smooth silky fur, and he liked to pluck wild grapes and feed them to him one by one. If a rock was too high for Christopher to scramble over, Arthur carried him, holding him tight against his chest. When they walked through tall grass, he put Christopher up on his shoulder so that Christopher could see which way to go. Being able to pick up his friend made Arthur feel strong.

They walked and walked. Arthur had never spent so much time outdoors. At home he had a yard with a sandbox and a swing set, and sometimes in the afternoons his mom made him go out there "to play." Arthur sat miserably in a lawn chair and waited for her to let him back in. Up the street he heard children shouting to each other. They sounded happy. He wanted to play with *them*. Sometimes he stood by the gate, hoping they would run past and speak to him. He even tried to open the gate and get out. But his mom saw out the kitchen window. She came and led him away from the gate. "I can't let you go too far," she'd said. "What if you needed your medicine?"

Arthur sighed. His mom was warm, and she smelled good, and she picked him up when he was tired and held him tight. Here the only one bigger than him was Margaret. She was nicer than she used to be, but she didn't realize that somebody was supposed to kiss him good night and sing him a song before he fell asleep. His dad knew. He thought his dad would come see them any day now.

He thought his mom probably wouldn't come. She didn't like small furry animals like Christopher. They'd seen one in the alley once, and she'd screamed and pulled Arthur in the other direction.

"What are you thinking?" Christopher grinned at Artie and settled himself on a cozy patch of moss. Sunlight streamed through the trees, and a chickadee twittered at them from a nearby bramble. Arthur

[138]

sat down, too. He hugged his knees to his chest and thought about what he would have liked to say. He opened his mouth. "Hungry."

"I thought so." Christopher divided a packet of dried corn and handed Arthur some wild grapes. "That ought to hold you for a while." They ate in silence. When he was done Christopher lay back and let his full belly poke up into the air.

"Did I tell you I always wanted a little brother? I told my mom, but she said I was enough for her to handle, and if there were two of us she didn't know what she'd do. My dad agreed with her. So I played a lot with my friends' little brothers. I'd teach them all kinds of stuff . . . like how to say the alphabet, and where the best berries grow, and how to make a ball out of a hickory nut." Christopher trailed off. He rolled onto his side and let his limbs stretch out on the soft moss. "There's so much I still have to learn about you, Artie. Like who your human friends are, and what you like to play with, stuff like that. And there's a lot here you haven't seen yet. In the fall the valley is beautiful. The leaves are red and orange and yellow, and we spend all day in the woods, picking up hazelnuts and chin-quapins and walnuts to store over the winter. For lunch we make a fire and roast some of the nuts we've found. And winter—winter's the best time of all. It snows, and we go sledding on the mountainside, and skating on Emerald Pond. Isabella makes big pots of soup, and for dessert she makes ice cream out of snow! Sometimes when it's really cold, we stay inside all day, reading and doing experiments."

Arthur noticed that Christopher had stopped talking. He looked worried.

"You're kind of big to come inside," he murmured, getting up. "But I'll figure something out."

Arthur felt uneasy. He knew Christopher had been unhappy the night he left the faucet on. And the day he tried to cross the stream on the rats' wooden bridge hadn't been a good day for Christopher, either. The bridge had shattered into bits, and Christopher had tried to fix it but he couldn't, and the old rat had come, the one who wore a patch over one eye. He'd said something to Christopher that Arthur couldn't hear. Another day Arthur had stepped on some of the broccoli by mistake. He was really sorry after it happened. He wanted to explain that broccoli looked different at home; it was little green bits, lying on a plate instead of standing up in the garden. But he couldn't figure out the words to say.

Arthur trotted down the path behind Christopher. A chickadee flew out of the thicket and landed on the mossy patch to search for crumbs.

"Everything will work out just fine," Christopher continued. "I'm a great problem solver, believe you me. If you think there is a problem, that is." He sighed, glanced at Arthur, and put on a bright smile.

"It's almost time for another meeting of the Brave Explorers Club, Christopher, President, Artie, Vice-President! We'll meet at the flat rock just by the bend in the stream. The meeting's at three o'clock sharp. Hurry! We have to get there on time!"

Chapter 16

"Over here," Margaret murmured. "Over here, Leon." She shifted on her bed of pine needles, then hugged her arms close for warmth. Leon was looking in the wrong place. When she spoke, he turned his head. She could see his thin brown face, his heavy glasses, his sharp eyes; he was so close she could almost touch him. "Here," she murmured again. Then she woke up.

It was still dark. She moved her head close to the door and lay on her back, looking up. The stars were strewn across the sky like flowers. She could pick out the North Star; Racso had shown her that. And the bright one to the east would be Venus, the evening star. When she was little she used to say a rhyme about it:

> Star light, star bright,
> First star I see tonight,
> I wish I may, I wish I might,
> Have the wish I wish tonight.

What is my wish? Margaret sighed. Where do I want to be? And who? Do I want to be with Leon, going to school and having fun? Do I want to be with Mom and Dad, in my own house? Do I want to be here, living in the hut with Artie? And what if I want *all* those things?

Whooooooo? Whooooooo? The voice drifted from someplace high on the mountain. I don't know who, Mr. Owl, Margaret thought wearily. She crawled back to her bed and fell asleep.

In the end she decided without really thinking it through. But first there were more days: days of digging up the sweet potato crop, days of harvesting wild grapes: mashing them, straining them, boiling the juice to make grape jelly. While she was working with Isabella, Margaret asked about the winter. "What will you do for food? And how will you keep warm?"

"We have wood to burn, of course. In fact we'll probably start cutting more next week. We keep some from the past year to start the green logs."

"Green?"

"Fresh-cut. It burns hotter and longer, but it's hard to get going."

"Won't you run out of trees?"

"We plant more each spring—pines and hardwoods: oak, locust, and hickory. That way we'll always have a supply. And as for food, that's why we're making this jelly. We'll end up with enough to last all winter."

"But you can't just eat jelly."

"We'll have potatoes, cabbages, apples, turnips, carrots, and onions in the cold cellar. We'll grind more flour in October, and we'll harvest the honey then, too. We'll dry apples and persimmons and beans inside their pods."

"You've got it all figured out. I mean, you know exactly what you need, and when you'll harvest it." Margaret couldn't keep the surprise out of her voice.

"Of course." Isabella was starting to get impatient. "Except that you two will probably eat us out of house and home this winter. Arthur seems to eat more every day."

That was true. Margaret had noticed that he was growing, not just taller but rounder, too. She mentioned it to Christopher, and he seemed pleased. "That just shows that this is the right place for Artie. I know how to take care of him better than anybody else."

"You don't take better care of him than my mom!" Margaret was surprised at the vehemence in her voice. "My mom did everything for Artie. She spent all day taking him to the doctors and the hospital for tests."

"I spend all day playing with him. That's what he likes."

"Well, how are you going to take care of him when it gets cold? Where's he going to live then?"

The questions hung in the air like something visible. Margaret shivered. She hadn't dared ask the questions about herself; but Artie was different. She had to take care of Artie. He was her brother.

Christopher looked scared, but his voice was calm. "I have a plan, believe me. Everything will work out fine."

Everything will work out fine. . . . Margaret repeated the phrase over and over as she labored in the wheatfield, cutting the tall stalks with a primitive stone blade. The rhythm of the work was soothing: bend and stroke, bend and stroke. A team of rats followed her, tying the wheat into bundles. Another team loaded the bundles onto a wood sledge, which was drawn back to the nest when it was full. Before she had come, it had taken ten rats, harnessed together, to pull the heavy sledge. But for Margaret it was easy.

Harvest was a wonderful time. Each day groups of rats set out in different directions, their tools

[145]

and baskets on their backs. At sunset they came back, bringing containers filled with nuts, apples, acorns, berries, herbs, and vegetables. The wheat was threshed on flat stones beside the creek. Sugar beets were ground into a fine sweet paste; and corn was shucked and hung in rows to dry. Racso supervised the making of peanut butter. Christopher and Arthur helped him shell the peanuts and put them in a hopper to be ground by stones that rubbed against each other. Arthur liked turning the crank and watching the wet, thick peanut butter come oozing out the chute. But one time he forgot to stop turning when Racso was adding more peanuts. Racso's paw got caught in the hopper. When he pulled it out, it was bleeding.

"AAAAAAAAAAH! Run get Elvira, quick!" He held the hurt paw tight to his belly. Someone had run for the doctor; other rats hurried from everywhere.

"What happened?"

Racso couldn't answer. Christopher stood beside him, trying to help.

"What happened, Christopher?" Isabella was there now, and here came Elvira, scurrying up the path with her bag full of medicine and bandages.

"It was an accident," Christopher said miserably. He didn't look at Arthur, who was sitting quietly on the ground.

"But how did it happen?"

"He got his paw caught in the grinder."

"But someone must have been turning the crank. The whetstones couldn't hurt you unless they were turning, and they don't turn unless someone is turning the—"

"Me did it," Arthur said in a lonely voice.

Everyone stared. Even Racso turned and looked at Arthur. It was the first time most of the rats had heard him speak.

"Me sorry," Arthur said. He got up slowly.

"I'm sure it will be okay, Artie," Christopher said quickly. "We all know it was an accident."

"Carelessness can cause terrible injuries," Elvira said. Her head was bent over Racso's paw. "This one will take a couple of weeks to heal, but it could have been worse."

"Ooooow. OOOOOOOOOOw!"

Arthur walked away, toward the pond. He started to cry. He wanted his mother to pick him up.

"It was an accident," Christopher said. "I was watching him, but I didn't realize he wasn't going to stop. I thought he knew."

The other rats looked at him.

"I'd better go after him," Christopher said. He did want to be with Arthur, but he also wanted to get away from Racso and the rest of the rats. He ran toward the pond. He found Artie sitting on the bank, sobbing.

"You didn't mean to do it," Christopher said.

But Arthur couldn't stop crying. Even the feel of warm fur against his face wasn't enough. He had hurt Racso! He was scared and confused and sorry. Most of all, he wanted his mother.

Margaret was in the wheatfield when the accident happened. No one told her. She kept working to the rhythm of her body: bend and stroke, bend and stroke. Behind her she heard Brendan and Sally chatting as they tied up the bundles. She heard the skidding of the sledge across the stubble of wheat, and the voices of the loaders. "Five o'clock," someone called.

She looked around. All but a small crescent of wheat had been cut. The sun was even with the crest of the mountains to the west. She signaled the rats to gather around.

"I think we could finish this in a half hour."

Brendan looked surprised. "We've put in a long day already."

"But to bring all the equipment out here tomorrow for a half hour's work doesn't seem worth it."

"She's right," somebody said. "If we finish to-night, we can start something else tomorrow."

"Okay." The rats went back to their places, and Margaret to her rhythm: bend and stroke. The wheat made a soft swish as it fell. The western sky was pink, and getting pinker. She moved easily; by now she was good at what she was doing. She imagined saying to Leon, "I cut a field of wheat." He'd think she was making it up, and he would laugh. She missed him badly, and her parents, too. Yet right now, with the sunset blooming to her left, the wheat falling softly, her body moving gracefully, the breeze drying the sweat on her arms and neck, she was happy.

She found out about Arthur when she got back. The rat who told her was reassuring: "Racso will have complete use of the paw when it's healed. And it should be as good as new in a month."

She didn't blame Artie; he was just a little kid. In fact he'd helped more in the valley than ever before. At home he used to sit around whining while everybody else did all the work, but here he'd become—she searched for the right word—*alive*. Now he wanted to help. Still, he'd hurt Racso, and that was on top of breaking the rats' bridge, and flooding the inside of their nest.

She shivered. Her arms were covered with goose bumps. The evenings were getting colder; last night she'd woken up in the dark, shivering. But these goose bumps . . . were they from cold? Or fear? I'll have to talk to Nicodemus, she thought. The wheatfield is all done, so I can go to him in the morning.

He looked as if he were expecting her. He was sitting on a stool in the pine grove, holding a piece of paper in his paw. He smiled as she drew near.

"I hear you all finished the wheat yesterday, and that you were the one who talked the rest of them into it."

She nodded, surprised that he knew.

"You've become someone whom the others listen to."

She felt a red flush creeping toward her face. "I *have* changed. I guess I never had to take care of things before. In a way I was like my parent's guest, just expecting them to take care of everything. And Artie was, too."

"Like a guest?"

She nodded. "Like a sick guest."

"You went to school. That must have been different."

She thought about it. "Not really. I did enough work to pass, but mostly I goofed off with my friend, Leon. He'd come up with all sorts of crazy ideas."

"Crazy ideas account for the advance of civilization. Galileo, Copernicus, Lister, Madame Curie . . . all crazy."

"How do you know about them?"

It was Nicodemus's turn to look embarrassed. "Sometimes I forget I haven't told you our history. I'll do that one day."

The silence between them was peaceful, and for a few moments Margaret didn't even think about the reason she'd come to see Nicodemus. She was about to bring up the subject of Artie when she noticed that the paper in Nicodemus's paw was a letter. So someone else did know about the rats! She couldn't keep from staring at it.

"Yes, it's a letter." Nicodemus answered the silent question. "It's from a friend of mine, Timothy Frisby. It's about you and Arthur."

"What does it say?"

"It says . . ." Nicodemus glanced at Margaret, then picked the letter up and read, " 'The missing children have been declared dead. A funeral service was held for them last week. Their parents—' "

"NO!" Margaret gasped. Her mother's face, her father's, flashed before her. They were filled with grief.

"We're going home!" she said. "I don't care how long it takes, or how far we have to walk. We're going home!"

Chapter 17

"Have you ever heard of a laboratory called NIMH?" Nicodemus asked quietly.

They had spent the time since Margaret's outburst talking about homes: the valley, the city where Nicodemus had been born, Margaret's home. They talked about what it would be like when she returned, and how much the rats would miss her, and Arthur, too.

"I don't think so." Margaret had the feeling Nicodemus was about to tell her something important.

"It's a place where they do experiments, to learn more about how animals and people think. It's in a city not far from yours."

"How do you know about it?"

Nicodemus paused. "I was there once. I, and eight others."

It took a moment for Margaret to understand. "You were in charge of an experiment?"

"No."

"Oh! You were . . . in a cage." The last part of the sentence came out in a whisper. The thought was too awful to be said out loud.

He nodded. "The experiment was run by a scientist, Dr. Schultz. We were given special shots to make us more intelligent. We learned a great deal, and from what we learned, we managed to escape. We fled in a group, ending up first at a farm and later at Thorn Valley. We left the farm for our own reasons, but we found out just before we did that Dr. Schultz was still looking for us. That was three years after we'd escaped."

"He must have wanted to find you really bad." Margaret looked at Nicodemus. She had the feeling there was something else he was trying to tell her. And then, suddenly, she understood.

"He's still looking for you," she said slowly.

"Yes. And he'll continue for the rest of his life."

"*Why?*"

"Because we're the missing piece in a puzzle he's spent years trying to solve. Without us, his life's work will remain unfinished."

"But he *won't* find you!" Margaret exclaimed.

[153]

"He'd never look in the valley unless someone told him . . ." She stopped. "Oh!" she said.

Nicodemus nodded slowly.

"I'll never tell! Never!"

"Keeping a secret can be hard."

"But I will! And I'll talk to Artie, too! He hardly ever says anything anyway."

"It's going to be hard," Nicodemus said. "Hard, and lonely. I know you'll do the best you can. But don't feel bad if—"

Margaret shook her head. "I won't tell!" She felt a glaze of tears against her eyes. "Never!"

Nicodemus promised the children they would have a guide to help them find their way home. They should leave by the end of the week, before the weather got colder. The journey would be hard, but not as hard as being lost, because they would know where they were going, and would have food. It would take them three days to reach a house where someone could call their parents to come and get them.

"That is, if the weather's good. If it rains, it will take longer. Rain is tough going for someone my age."

Margaret was only half listening. Something was bothering her. It was as if their departure had been planned before she ever opened her mouth.

"Would you have sent us away even if we wanted to stay?"

Nicodemus met her gaze sadly. "You couldn't have survived here over the winter. There might have been enough food—just enough—but we couldn't have built a shelter that would keep you warm. Justin and I talked about it, of course. Then, too, there was the—"

"The secret."

"That's right."

"So it wasn't anything I did—or Artie did?"

"Certainly not. We've accomplished so much with your help. Arthur, of course, is a different story. . . ." Nicodemus smiled. "It's been a pleasure to get to know you both."

"You know, Artie's really changed since he's been here. At home he never talked. My mom was going crazy worrying about him, with that, and the asthma, too. But here, he sort of . . . woke up."

"Yes. I've noticed. And Christopher's mentioned it, too."

The way Margaret felt before she asked the next question made her realize how much closer she felt to Artie. There was something about the way he'd been lately—not the trouble he'd caused, but the way he walked around with a kind of slaphappy grin on his face—that made her feel really good. And she didn't want that to go away. "Do you think they'll ever see each other again?"

"I think so, though I'm not sure when. There's

a lot of planning to do. We have a long trip ahead of us."

Margaret thought she hadn't heard right. "We?"

He nodded. "I'm going to be your guide."

"But you have trouble walking! Even if I carry you over the mountain, you might not be able to get back on your own."

"I'm not going to come back."

"*What?*"

"I'll explain later." And that was all Nicodemus would say.

She walked back to the hut to look for Arthur. On the way she passed Brendan, who was digging parsnips. He waved and called to her. She smiled, but she couldn't help thinking, he doesn't know I'm leaving. Nobody knows, except Nicodemus.

Arthur wasn't at the hut, nor was he at the flat rock where they'd started threshing, nor sitting by the pond. She started up the path toward the mountain and saw, in the distance, Arthur and Christopher meandering through the meadow. Christopher was sitting on the boy's shoulder. Goldenrod and Queen Anne's lace surrounded them like a yellow-and-white blanket. Margaret took a deep breath. She wondered if Artie would ever be this happy again.

She told him after dinner, when they were sitting together in the hut. Arthur was playing with his willow whistle.

"Do you remember the toys in your bedroom at home? Your Mickey Mouse doll, and your plastic golf set?"

Arthur looked at her intently. He nodded.

"Would you like to play with them again? Would you like to have hamburgers and candy bars and ice cream? Would you like to see Bambi and Dumbo on the VCR?"

Arthur couldn't think about those things. "Mommy," he whispered.

"You're going to see Mommy and Daddy soon, Artie. In a few days we're going home."

Arthur just sat there staring, as if he didn't know what to think. Then he started crying, but softly— not the loud wailing Margaret had expected. He clutched his whistle to his chest.

"Maybe you can take it with you, to remind you of Christopher and the valley. But we won't be able to talk about them to anybody else—not ever. It would be dangerous for them."

Arthur nodded as if he understood. He cried until he fell asleep.

In the morning Christopher could tell something was wrong. Arthur looked as if he'd been crying.

[157]

And he didn't grin when Christopher jumped into his lap.

"What's wrong, Artie?"

"Mommy."

"Do you miss your mommy? Try to think about the fun things we're going to do today. You and I are going to build a little dam. Would you like that?"

"Artie go home."

"It's too far. And you might get lost. Remember when you and Margaret were lost, and you had to—"

"You come, too."

"I can't, and you can't either, because it's too far."

Christopher didn't see Margaret, who had come up the path with a bowl of water in each hand. But she had heard the conversation.

"He is going home, Christopher. We're leaving Friday."

"What are you talking about?"

She didn't try to keep the sadness out of her voice. "We don't fit here—not forever. We would freeze in the winter without a house, and in the meantime we'd use up all the food. We're just . . . too big."

"You're not. *Artie's* not!"

"We are too. Even Nicodemus thinks so."

"Nicodemus!" Christopher spoke the name as if it were a bad word. "How can he say that!?"

[158]

"He didn't really—not until I told him I wanted to go back anyway. It was my idea."

"But that's crazy! You'll get lost again! And you'd need a guide, and food!"

"We have a guide." Margaret was firm. "It's all set. Like I said, we're leaving Friday. And Nicodemus is leaving with us."

Chapter 18

The next day Nicodemus called a meeting and told the rats the news. He named Justin and Beatrice the new leaders, and asked everyone to help them during the months after his departure.

"The scientists at NIMH thought they had made us immortal," he said sadly. "But they were wrong about that. Each of us will die."

Racso shook his head. He couldn't think about that, not with Nicodemus standing there full of life. But the old rat continued.

"Ever since I was little, I've dreamed of seeing the ocean. Lately that dream has become more powerful. Sometimes at night I think I hear the water

splashing against the sand, and the sea gulls calling. I smell the salt air. But when I wake up, I'm here, and the dream is gone.

"I had given up on it. Then I realized that Margaret and Arthur needed a guide to cross the mountain. If I were that guide, Margaret could carry me. By the time I reached Fitzgibbon's farm, the hardest part of my journey would be over."

"I don't want you to go." A small rat standing near the front spoke suddenly, as if she couldn't contain herself any longer.

"I want to go." His voice was grave. "But I will miss you all."

"Will you come back?"

Nicodemus didn't answer the question. Instead he patted one of the baby rats on the head, as if it were just another day.

Racso closed his eyes tight, as if that would make the whole scene disappear. Nicodemus wouldn't leave! He couldn't! Racso needed him! And for Margaret and Arthur to go at the same time! It was as if the world were being turned upside down. But as bad as it was for Racso, it was worse for Christopher.

Racso knew what it was like to lose someone you really cared about. He remembered when he'd found out his father had died: All he could do was lie on the ground and cry. So he stayed nearby while Christopher wept about Arthur, and when his friend shouted angrily that it was unfair, that they should have listened to *him*, he didn't argue.

"This is all wrong!" Christopher shouted. "Wrong! Wrong! Wrong!"

Racso listened.

"I found Arthur! I'm the one who should decide what happens to him! He's *mine*!"

Racso listened.

"I'm going, too!" Christopher shrieked. "I'm going with them! I'm not staying here by myself!"

A bit later he opened his eyes and looked at Racso.

"I don't want to leave here," he sobbed. "I've always lived here! My friends are here! This is my home!"

"You don't have to leave," Racso said gently. "We don't want you to."

Christopher and Arthur were inseparable for the next two days. They slept together in the hut, Christopher curled in a ball on Arthur's chest. They waded in the brook, picked wildflowers, ate bread and honey, looked for surprises under the oak tree.

They held three meetings of the Brave Explorers. The first two were about what to do that day and what to have for supper. Christopher tried to act like nothing had changed, but it was hard. Twice he blinked back tears, and Arthur looked stricken, too. But the third meeting was different. When Christopher called it to order, his voice was almost cheery.

"Agenda item number one," he announced. "Trip."

Artie waited.

"I'm not talking about your trip," Christopher said.

Artie waited.

"I'm talking about another trip. Because I've made a decision, Artie—a very grown-up decision. I've decided that no matter how I feel about it, I'm going to have to say good-bye to you tomorrow. Racso and I talked, and I realized I wouldn't want to be away from my mom and dad forever, either. Not only that, but the winters here are cold. Racso said children wear thick jackets in cold weather. And we don't have one for you.

"But I couldn't stand the idea that I would never see you again." Christopher gulped. "Like I told you, I'd always dreamed about having a little brother. Then I found you. I can't just say good-bye forever. And that's what the trip is about."

"What?" Arthur's eyes were big.

"I'm coming to visit you in the city. Racso's coming with me, so I won't get lost. I'll come when the leaves change color."

Arthur clapped his hands.

"I'm going to tell Nicodemus tonight. Well, I'm going to ask him, really. But I'm pretty sure he'll say it's okay."

Arthur started jumping up and down. He couldn't wait for Christopher to come to his house.

"The meeting's not adjourned yet." Christopher waited while Arthur sat back down. "We still have to vote on this. Now, raise your hand if you want me to visit you. Let's see—that's one vote, and I make two. Anyone opposed? No. The ayes have it! HOORAY!"

Before Christopher got the chance to go see Nicodemus, he got a message that Nicodemus wanted to see *him* in his office. To his surprise Racso was in the office, too. Nicodemus gestured for them to sit down.

"I've talked to Margaret about NIMH," he began. "She's volunteered to keep our identity a secret."

"I think she will," Racso said eagerly. "Kids love secrets. Remember last year when I taught everyone the backward code? All the kids—"

Christopher shot a glance at Racso that said: Pipe down.

"Secrets can be fun, when they're shared," Nicodemus said. "But they can also be lonely."

"Margaret will have Artie to talk to. And we can

help her make up a great story about what happened to her." Racso waved his paws. "Like how she saved Artie from bobcats and rattlesnakes! How she fed him beetles and tadpoles and worms to keep him alive! She'll be like Tarzan!"

"That might work for a little while. But I think people will question her story."

"Then she can make up something else! She can say she met a lonely wolf and he took them into his cave and fed them. But they missed their parents, so they decided to go back."

Nicodemus shook his head. "I think her story needs to be simple. I'll try to work it out with her on the trip. But telling a story—and sticking to it— can be hard."

Christopher sat up straight. He started to open his mouth to say something important, but Nicodemus silenced him. "Just a minute. I have a proposal to make. And don't think it will be easy." He looked hard at both of them.

"I think the two of you should visit the children. The visit will have to be brief—just a day. You can't take the risk of being caught or seen with them. But you'll be able to let them know we still care about them. And if they haven't been able to keep the secret, we'll know."

"I . . . I . . ." Christopher stared. "That was my idea."

"Good. So you want to go?"

"Yes!"

"What about you, Racso?"

Racso snatched his beret off his head and dusted it off, as if the trip were starting today. "Certainly. I know how to get around in the city. And I'll take good care of Christopher."

Christopher wanted to shout: Nobody has to take care of me! But he noticed Nicodemus looking right at him. He swallowed.

"You're to bring a report back to Justin and Beatrice."

"We will."

"You'll be careful, won't you?" Nicodemus looked at them fondly. "I won't be around to help if you get into trouble."

"We'll be careful."

They got up, but Racso couldn't just leave. "I'll always remember you, Nicodemus. And I'll miss you—a lot."

"Me, too," Christopher whispered.

Nicodemus didn't answer, but he put a paw on each of their heads.

Christopher left the office feeling sad and happy and excited and scared and already lonely.

They left the next morning. Someone had fashioned a wicker basket for Margaret to wear on her back. It held food and a bed for Nicodemus. All the rats watched as she placed him in the basket and fastened it on. Margaret wasn't sure what to say. Leaving the rats felt like leaving everything she had: her house that she'd built herself, her wooden plate, her pine-needle mattress, her meadow filled with flowers, her life. The rats crowded around her legs, making her feel like Paul Bunyan. She gripped Arthur's hand tight. "Thanks for taking care of us," she said weakly.

"Things didn't start off so well between us, but they ended up better," Isabella said. "We'll miss you."

Margaret nodded. She wanted to say: I don't want to go.

"Thanks for moving the nest," Isabella added. "And for helping with the dam, and cutting the wheat, and everything else."

Margaret's throat ached. She tried to memorize the picture of the rats standing by the nest, the garden stretching behind them, the mountains beyond that. She took a step. Then it hit Arthur that he wouldn't see Christopher again for a long, long time. He sank to the ground.

"Get up, Artie."

He shook his head.

"You have to get up," Margaret said. "We're leaving."

Arthur pointed to Christopher.

"He can't come. I told you that already, remember? We're going home."

Arthur began to cry, and then Margaret began to cry, too. The tears rolled down her face. Arthur wasn't going to walk away and pretend that it was okay to be leaving, because it wasn't okay. It was awful.

It was Christopher who saved the day. He climbed into Arthur's lap and stood up on his hind legs so that his furry face was staring right into Arthur's face. He licked Arthur right on the nose. Arthur couldn't keep on crying while he was being licked, so he began to laugh. Christopher whispered something in his ear. Arthur hiccuped and wiped his eyes.

And then they went through the meadow, and over the log across the stream, and up the stony path to the mountain.

Chapter 19

"Tell me what to say," Margaret whispered. She whispered because it was dark, and Arthur was asleep by the campfire just a few feet away. They had walked all day, crossing the peak of the mountain in midafternoon. They had chosen a knoll beside a clump of cedars for their camp. There had been sandwiches made by Isabella for dinner, but Arthur began nodding off before his was finished.

"Begin with the things that really happened," Nicodemus said. "You must stay as close to the truth as you can, without mentioning us. Remember that a lot of what you ate and your shelter grew naturally in the valley."

"We decided to go for a walk together while Mom

was taking a nap. We crossed over a hill and were following an old logging road when we suddenly saw a bear! We started running, and that's when we got lost."

Nicodemus nodded.

So she told the whole story as if it had really happened. Nicodemus asked her questions, and she tried to think up answers that fit. Then he questioned the answers. It was hard. There were always things that Margaret hadn't thought about, like how she got a fire started, and how she knew which plants were poisonous. She got frustrated.

"I'm not sure I can do this. What if they don't believe me?"

"Just repeat what you said before. And be careful not to change your story. That would arouse suspicion." Nicodemus sighed. "I don't feel good about this. But I'm afraid the well-being of the others depends on it."

"I'll do it," Margaret said. "And I'll talk to Artie about it tomorrow."

For breakfast there were peanut butter sandwiches with raisins in them, and plums, and apple tarts. Nicodemus measured where the sun came over the cliff before he told Margaret which way to go. They walked all day, crossing a ridge and coming down into a thick wood. That night they camped in a little valley. Margaret wanted to make a fire, but

Nicodemus said no, that they were only five miles from a ranger's lookout tower. Margaret felt funny, knowing that another human was that close. She wondered how she'd feel, seeing people again. She shivered.

Before dinner she told Arthur the story she planned to tell when they got back: that they'd been frightened by the bear and wandered away, over the mountain. They'd lived in a cave and then built a hut while they waited to be found. They'd lived off berries and fish and wild grapes and birds' eggs, and she'd concocted a medicine for Arthur made from herbs that grew along the banks of the stream. After a time they'd given up hope of being found. They'd packed food and started walking. After days and days, they'd come upon a house. . . .

"Remember we're not going to tell anyone about the rats," Margaret said.

I'm not going to tell anyone about anything, Arthur thought. He missed Christopher already.

"We don't want anyone to know about the rats," Margaret repeated. "Get it, Artie?"

Arthur nodded. He wondered what was going to happen.

Margaret fixed supper. She tried not to think about the fact that this was the last evening she would spend with Nicodemus. Leaving the valley had been bad enough; having him with them had made it easier. But tomorrow he would leave too. They would be found and go back home. Racso and Christopher might visit, but Nicodemus would become a memory.

Her hands shook as she unwrapped the food and set it on clean broad leaves, then dipped water from the stream to go with it.

"You're nervous," Nicodemus said.

"Not nervous," she snapped. "Hungry."

But she wasn't hungry. The food tasted like sawdust, and swallowing was painful. Margaret couldn't look Nicodemus in the face. She couldn't think of anything to say. She looked down at her hands and saw her fingernails, black with grime. When kids came to school dirty, the teacher sent a note home to their parents. But Nicodemus didn't care about dirt. He cared about adventures, dreams, and feelings.

After Artie fell asleep, they sat together in the dark. Nicodemus seemed to know what she'd been thinking.

"It's going to be a change, isn't it?" he asked softly.

She shrugged. "I'll get used to it. I have no choice."

"Maybe you do," he answered pleasantly. "When I first met you, you wanted to go back."

"That was before I got used to being on my own. I liked building my house, and working for my food. I even liked climbing the cliff. After I did it, that is. It made me feel . . ." She hesitated, trying to find the right word. "Real."

"You were real before that."

"I know. But it didn't feel like it."

Nicodemus turned toward her. "This will be the first time I've gone off on my own since before NIMH. I don't know what it will be like."

Margaret was surprised. "Are you scared?"

"Yes."

"Me, too," Margaret said.

They stretched out on the ground beside Arthur. Looking up through the trees, Margaret could see a crescent of moon hanging in the dark.

"Nicodemus," she whispered.

"Yes?"

"The moon is getting smaller. In a week or so it won't be there at all."

"It will be there. You just won't be able to see it."

"Is it true, what you said about yourself? That you're going . . ." She couldn't bring herself to finish the question.

"To die?" He paused. "Yes."

"I don't want you to."

He sighed.

"I don't," she said again. But he didn't answer.

Before he left, Nicodemus showed them the way: down the hill to an old logging road, then right.

Then he went off into the brush, his cane in one paw. For a while she and Arthur just stood there, staring at the spot where he had disappeared. Margaret held Arthur's hand tight, and they started down the road.

After a while they came to a farmhouse. They climbed the porch steps and knocked on the door. A boy about her age answered it. He stared at her as if she were from another planet. Margaret was suddenly aware of her grimy, raggedy sweatshirt, and the streaks of dirt on Arthur's face. The boy looked as if he were about to slam the door.

"Could I use the telephone?" Margaret asked. Her voice felt thin.

"MOM!" the boy shouted. He didn't take his eyes off Margaret.

A woman in a flowered housedress appeared behind the boy. Her face changed when she saw them.

"I'd like to use the telephone," Margaret repeated. "We've been lost, and I want to call my parents."

"You can't be the two . . ." The woman's eyes traveled from Margaret's face down to her shoes, then over Arthur, head to foot. "Heavens!" she exclaimed, and in the same breath, "Billy, run fetch your dad!" She opened the door and herded Margaret and Arthur inside. "Come in, come in."

The room was bright and pretty, with floral chair covers and a red rocker beside the woodstove. But all Margaret could think was, I'm in a house again, where people live.

"Come sit here," the woman said. "Sit down. I'll get you something to eat." She gestured to a wooden table with a pitcher of flowers on it. Then the door opened and a man in denim overalls came striding in, the boy at his heels. He towered over the children, staring down at them with steel-blue eyes. But his voice was gentle.

"Your name?"

"Margaret Livingstone."

"And you?"

"His name's Arthur," Margaret said quickly.

"Where did you come from?"

"From the woods—out that way. We got lost a long time ago, and we couldn't find our way back to the campsite."

"I know," the man interrupted hastily. "I know all about that. But we thought . . ." He stopped and looked over at his wife. "We had given up hope."

"We were gone a long time," Margaret murmured.

"I have cookies for you," the woman said. "And milk. Here, on the table."

They were Oreo cookies. Margaret's hands were shaking. The man dialed the telephone.

"Sheriff Johnson, right away." He couldn't stop looking at them. "Yes, it's Paul Fitzgibbon. Those children who were lost . . . Yes, yes in Northwoods

[176]

. . . they're here! They're at my place! I'm sure! I'm sure!"

In a moment he hung up the phone. "Sheriff's coming out," he told Margaret. "He wants to see you with his own eyes before he calls your folks."

"Poor things." The woman stood beside Margaret and put one hand on her shoulder. "What a nightmare they've been through."

Something about the warm hand touching her made Margaret feel funny, and before she knew it she was crying, the tears streaming down her face and onto the front of her dirty sweatshirt. Arthur sat at the table, his eyes like little owl eyes, and watched Margaret cry.

Chapter 20

They didn't know until they were folded in their
mother's arms, smelling the powder on her neck,
hearing her say their names over and over, that
they were back. Their dad blew his nose and cried.
Someone gave him another handkerchief, and he
laughed, and then he cried again. Margaret let him
carry her to the car. She lay in the backseat with
her eyes closed, resting, being back.

They went right to the hospital, to make sure
they were okay. Then Margaret told the story, just
as she had practiced it with Nicodemus. Their questions weren't as hard as his, but she was glad when
they stopped asking. Her dad and a doctor talked

to the press: Both the children were in good condition, considering their ordeal, and amazingly, Arthur's asthma seemed cured. Flashbulbs popped. People were laughing and shouting, as if they were at a big party. Still, Margaret felt scared. What if they didn't believe her?

Then it was over. They were whisked out a side door. But a red-haired woman was waiting there.

"Of course I remember you," her mom said. "You helped us during the search." They spoke together for a moment. "Call us in a few days," her mom said.

"Who was that?"

"Lindsey Scott. She's a reporter—but I'll tell you about that later. Now it's time to go home."

Home was wonderful: soft corduroy chairs and thick rugs and cookies and soda and comic books and stuffed animals and brand-new slippers for both of them. Margaret had a bath. She couldn't believe the dark brown of her body against the white tub. Her legs were covered with scrapes and bruises she'd hardly noticed in the valley. When she shampooed her hair, she felt like Santa Claus with a huge mane of bubbles. She dabbed perfume and bath oil and aftershave lotion all over and then wrapped herself in a thick bathrobe. Her dad had bought a video of Walt Disney cartoons, and she and Arthur sat on the sofa, eating popcorn and drinking hot chocolate. They didn't talk about what had happened, or about what would happen later. They fell asleep on the sofa, both of them, and their parents carried them upstairs and put them to bed.

Arthur spent the next day in his pajamas, eating M&M's and playing with all the stuff in his toybox. There were toys in there he'd forgotten about! Like his Hop-Along Teddy, and the driving set with lights that really flashed when you moved the turn signal. Christopher would love that! Christopher didn't have many toys. He had a wooden ball and a stick to hit it with, and a doll bed made from a nutshell. He had paper and blue ink and purple ink, and a headband made of mica, and a top made from an acorn. Arthur held his Hop-Along Teddy in his lap and stroked its woolly fur. Christopher was far away now. He was a secret, like the secret in the closet. But he'd said he would come.

The doorbell rang. Arthur jumped up and ran to see who it was. But it was only Leon, Margaret's friend.

"Come in, Leon. Margaret's upstairs. I'll tell her you're here." Their mom gave Leon a hug. "Isn't this wonderful?"

"Yes, Mrs. Livingstone." Leon managed to wriggle out and stood looking at the carpet.

"Hi!" Margaret smiled at him from the upstairs landing. "Come on up! I've been waiting for you!"

"Right." Leon climbed the steps two at a time. When he got into her room, Margaret saw that he was taller. She felt shy. She thought of the hundreds of conversations she'd had with Leon when he wasn't there. She sat down on the bed.

"Hi."

"Hi," she repeated.

"I saw you on TV after you called. You and Artie were on every channel. They even interrupted the ball game with a special bulletin."

"Yeah." Margaret smiled. She'd been on television! Everyone would have seen her! But Leon didn't seem too excited about that. He was standing with his hands in his pockets. "What happened while I was gone?"

Margaret had intended the question to be about her—about what the kids had said when she was lost. But Leon didn't answer it that way. Instead he said, "Gram died."

"Oh!"

"She had a stroke."

"A stroke . . ." It had never occurred to Margaret that anything would have changed while she was gone. She and Nicodemus hadn't talked about that. She didn't know what to say. "I . . . I never thought . . ."

"That's okay," Leon mumbled. "She was really old, you know."

[181]

Margaret felt awful. She tried to change the subject. "How's school?"

"Okay. The kids held a memorial service for you, and lots of the girls were crying: Elinor and Patty and Roseanne."

"What did you do for your birthday?"

"Oh." Leon shifted from one foot to the other. "Hal and Tammy and I went to Glynn Falls. I rode the Cyclops twelve times."

"You went to Glynn Falls Amusement Park with *Tammy*?" Margaret thought they'd agreed that Tammy was a jerk. Furthermore, Leon usually spent his birthday with her, Margaret! She glared. "Didn't you mind that I was gone?"

"Of course I did." Leon frowned.

"Well, I missed you. Sometimes in my mind I talked to you."

"What did you say?"

"Oh, just things about what was happening. I was lonely, and scared, too. And I couldn't say that to Artie."

"You look different." Leon was staring. "Your face is tan and your hair's long and you're not as fat as you were."

"I *wasn't* fat." She would have liked to tell Leon about the rats, who tried to get as fat as they could during the fall, in case they had a hard winter. Christopher was hoping to turn into a little gray ball. She tried to shift her thoughts, but Leon broke in.

"On TV they said you knew how to eat in the wilderness from watching the Euall Gibbons show. I started laughing. Remember how we used to poke fun at that old guy?"

"I guess some of it soaked in anyway," Margaret said uneasily. "That happens, you know."

He looked at her doubtfully.

"I learned a lot of things just by being there," Margaret said to fill the silence. "I built a hut for Artie and me to sleep in. I even climbed a cliff."

"Why would you want to do that?"

"I . . . I wanted to look in a hawk's nest, to see if there were any eggs we could eat."

"How could you get the eggs down without breaking them?"

"I lowered them down in my sweatshirt, with a rope made of vines."

"How did you make the rope?"

"I figured it out—"

"The whole thing sounds like Wonder Woman or something," Leon interrupted. "It just doesn't sound like you."

"I changed, I guess. I had to."

Leon didn't say anything.

"The valley is so beautiful." Margaret's voice felt weak. "There are mountains on both sides, and a creek runs through a field covered with flowers. It's like something you'd see on TV, except it's real." She broke off.

"It sounds pretty," Leon said. But he was still looking at her like he didn't believe her. "I want you to tell me more about it," he said slowly. "Like what you did all day—stuff like that."

"Okay." Margaret shrugged, as if that would be easy. She thought of the wheatfield and the dam, but of course she couldn't tell about those. She opened her mouth, hoping the right words would come out, but nothing happened.

"What's the matter?"

"Nothing. It's just that I'm a little tired right now, and it's hard for me to think about . . . being lost and all. I'll tell you another time."

"When?"

"Tomorrow, maybe?"

"Sure."

Leon hung around for a while longer, even though Margaret felt really uncomfortable. She'd never felt that way around him before. He seemed to sense it, too; but he wouldn't give up.

"I read *The Swiss Family Robinson* this summer. That's about a whole family that gets shipwrecked on an island. They have to build their own house and plant crops and catch fish and everything—sort of like you and Artie."

"Yeah."

"You will tell me about it, right? I really want to know."

"Sure," Margaret said. Her throat felt dry.

"Tomorrow, right?"

"Yeah." She nodded.

But she knew she could not.

Chapter 21

The day the reporter called about the interview was the same day Margaret went back to school. The telephone rang during breakfast. Her mom held one hand over the mouthpiece and said, "It's that reporter, Lindsey Scott—remember, we met her as we were leaving the press conference? She'd like to interview you, Margaret."

"I don't know." Margaret's mouth was full of toast, and her mind was on school. "Maybe."

"She's awfully nice. She says it wouldn't be a long interview—maybe twenty minutes, this Friday evening. What do you think?"

It was easier—and less suspicious—to say yes. Margaret nodded. "Okay."

Her mom got directions. She hung up the phone and came over to Margaret. "It must be hard, going back to school after all that's happened. But after this interview Friday, we'll put the past behind us. We'll settle down and be like we used to be." She put her hand on Margaret's shoulder.

"I don't know if I'll ever be like I used to be," Margaret said. It was hard to swallow her toast.

"You'll always be my dear, sweet Margaret," her mom said. "Always."

"You look *good*," Elinor Huber said at lunchtime. "You've got a great tan, and you've lost weight, too; haven't you?"

"I guess so." Part of Margaret felt like saying, What business is it of yours? On the other hand, Elinor was the most popular girl in the whole school.

"You can sit at our table if you want to," Elinor said. She flipped a lock of her wavy blond hair over her shoulder.

Margaret hesitated. Usually she sat with Leon. But she was nervous that he'd ask more questions about the valley.

"Come on," Elinor said. "You can tell us about your summer." She made it sound like Margaret had been away on a cruise. Margaret worried that they might ask questions, too, but they hardly asked anything. Mostly they talked about TV shows and movie stars and what they were going to wear to school the next day. They had on pastel jogging suits with a parrot insignia on the right sleeve. Margaret found out that Elinor never ate her dessert. If no one else wanted it, she threw it in the trash. Margaret wanted it, but she felt funny about saying so. She also felt funny about Leon, who was sitting at another table with Tammy.

"How come you sat with Elinor at lunch?" Leon asked. He was sitting on the chair in her bedroom, kicking one of his hightops against the other.

"I don't know. I guess I just wanted to see what she was like. How come you sat with Tammy?"

Leon ignored the question. "Elinor only likes you because you're famous," he said. "Last year she said you were disgusting."

"You're just saying that because I didn't sit with you."

"No, I'm not." Leon raised two fingers. "Scouts' honor. She did say it, but I didn't tell you because I didn't want to hurt your feelings. She said it after you broke her Barbie doll. Anyway, Tammy's my friend now. She's okay when you get to know her. At least she's not a phony like Elinor."

Margaret glared at Leon, and he scowled back. She'd thought he'd be glad to have her back, and now he was acting like this. "I'll bet you didn't even miss me!" Margaret spat the words out.

"Don't be stupid."

"I'm not being stupid."

"I did miss you, but now I wonder why. You act like you're not my friend."

"What do you mean?"

"Like eating lunch with Elinor. And you don't want to tell me what happened to you."

"Oh." Margaret felt trapped. She didn't want to lie to Leon, but she couldn't tell him the truth, either. "I just don't want to talk about it," she said lamely.

"Why not? You talked to Elinor about it. I heard you, at lunchtime."

"Sure, I talked to her a bit. But that doesn't mean what I said was true."

Leon stared at Margaret. "What do you mean?"

"What I mean is, if I could tell you everything, I would."

"Why can't you?"

"Because somebody else might get hurt."

Leon ran one hand through his curly hair. "If you told me?"

She nodded.

"Who?"

"I can't say."

"Is this another one of your stories?"

"It's for real. I swear."

"But I wouldn't tell anybody."

"I know. But I promised."

"I'm supposed to be your best friend." Leon was indignant. "You should be loyal, and you shouldn't keep secrets."

"I can't tell you," Margaret said flatly. "I just can't."

Arthur was with the secret when he heard his mom coming. He scrambled out from under the eaves of the closet and sat down in the middle of a pile of toys. When she came in he was playing with his wooden train. She sat down beside him.

"Tomorrow you're going to nursery school," she said softly. "There will be lots of children and toys to play with. Before, I was afraid to let you go, but you're so much better . . ." She smiled. "I wish you could tell me what it was like in the valley," she said. "Margaret made it sound beautiful."

Arthur looked at his mom. Didn't she know he wasn't supposed to tell about the rats? Margaret had made him promise. And what was nursery school?

"I bought you a new outfit for your first day at school." His mom showed him a green shirt and a pair of red overalls with trains on them. He liked trains.

"Not today," she said, taking them gently out of his hands. "Tomorrow."

Arthur frowned. He wanted them *now*.

"You're going to love it," his mom said, smiling.

The next morning his mom brought the overalls and shirt into his bedroom again. She helped him put them on. Then they got into the car and headed for nursery school. But as they turned the corner beyond the house, Arthur thought of something. What if Christopher came while he was gone? He wouldn't know when Arthur was coming back. Maybe he would just leave. Arthur looked at his mom. Maybe she could tell Christopher that he would be back soon. But no—she wasn't supposed to know about Christopher. It was all so confusing. He started to whine.

"We're almost there . . . we just turn this way . . ." His mom patted him on the leg. "Here it is."

They walked past a playground to a stone building with a red door. When the door opened, Arthur saw children everywhere: sitting at low tables, climbing on a red jungle gym, playing with blocks on the floor. A woman in blue jeans came over and squatted down beside him. He held on to his mom's hand.

"I'm Teresa," she said. "I'll help you find something to play with. And then you can meet a few of the children."

I want to go home! Arthur thought. But he couldn't help noticing a large yellow dump truck filled with sand.

His mom let go his hand, but she gave him a

kiss and said, "I'll sit over in the corner while you get used to things."

Arthur shook his head. He sat down on the rug and closed his eyes.

The next day his mom didn't stay at nursery school. Arthur cried for a few moments after she left. Teresa held him on her lap. Then the other children came to the table for snack. They were having Hawaiian Punch and peanut butter crackers. Teresa put a paper cup filled with punch in front of Arthur, but he wouldn't touch it. He swallowed. Hawaiian Punch was really good. He jammed his hands into his pants pockets. If he drank the punch, that would mean he wanted to be here.

Later they played with toys. Arthur sat on the rug and watched. A boy called Stevie was playing with the yellow truck. The truck had a lifter on the front, and Stevie would lift sand out of the sandbox and dump it on a plastic mat. Once he noticed Arthur watching him. He pushed the truck across the rug so it almost touched Arthur's shoe. Then it did touch the shoe. Bump! Bump! Arthur moved his foot. The truck had a black stick, like a gearshift. It seemed real.

"I'm having an interview with a newspaper reporter tonight," Margaret told Elinor at lunch on Friday. "She's dying to meet me."

"You should have told me yesterday," Elinor said. "I could have helped you with your hair. What are you going to wear?"

"I hadn't really thought about that."

Elinor rested her chin in the palm of one hand. "Let's see now . . . you have the turquoise pants— they're out; then the purple ones . . ." She paused, shook her head. "Your jeans are too casual. You never come to school in a dress, but I suppose you must have at least two or three at home. What are they like?"

"I don't think I want to wear a dress." Margaret actually did have one dress in her closet, which she had worn to her cousin's wedding. It was red. She hated it.

"Is there time for your mom to take you shopping?" Elinor sounded really concerned. "If I were you, I'd look for the new dropped-waist dresses with stripes. I think they'd do the most for your figure."

"I don't think I want to wear a dress," Margaret repeated. She clenched her teeth. She was sorry she'd brought the whole thing up. Across the room she could see Leon and Tammy bent over a book. Leon pointed at something on the page, and they both laughed. They looked like they were having fun.

That night Margaret and Artie went with their Mom to meet Lindsey Scott. She'd been in the valley, too! She showed them photographs of the creek and the field where the pine trees grew.

"I was in Thorn Valley on a canoe trip two years ago," she explained. "A ranger and I went there when a dam was being built at the north end. We took pictures because we wanted to show the public what would be lost if the land were flooded. Luckily, the plan to build the dam was abandoned." She smiled as she sifted through the pictures. "It's the most beautiful place I've ever been. This is where we ate lunch that day. Does it look familiar?"

"I don't think so." Margaret pushed her hands against her knees to keep them from shaking. She felt tricked. No one had told her Lindsey Scott had been in the valley. She didn't want to look at the pictures, but she couldn't help seeing the little beach near Emerald Pond, with the walnut tree behind it, and the mountains behind that. It made her feel so homesick. She swallowed. She tried to keep her face expressionless, the way she would if she were hiding something from the teacher at school. "I don't recognize those places," she said.

"Really?" Lindsey was disappointed, and surprised, too. Margaret didn't seem interested in the pictures. And her tone of voice reminded Lindsey of phrases she'd had to memorize as a child: "I had a good time at the party, Homer," or "Thanks for the socks, Grandma. They were just what I wanted."

Margaret realized she had to say something. "We got our drinking water from a creek," she said. "And we caught crayfish and frogs there, too. I made a fire on the beach and cooked them over hot stones."

"How did you know to do that?"

Margaret almost smiled with relief. She'd practiced this question with Nicodemus. "I'd seen people do it at a clambake on Cape Cod a couple of years ago."

"Did you ever see signs of civilization in the valley?"

Margaret shook her head.

Lindsey persisted. "Like Indian arrowheads, or old soda bottles, or anything that might suggest people had been there?"

Margaret shook her head again. "I thought I heard a helicopter once, but then the sound went away. I didn't know it was real until my dad told me they had flown helicopters on the other side of the mountain range."

Lindsey leaned forward. "I had a strange experience when I was in the valley," she confided. "After we paddled up the creek, we ate lunch at the beach I showed you in the picture. I bent over afterward to rinse my hands, and I found something in the sand." She paused. "It was a little basket, about four inches long, with straps attached to it. It was beautifully made, and it hadn't rotted a bit, so it couldn't have been there long. We thought it must have been a child's toy."

"Where is it now?" Margaret's voice was hushed.

Lindsey sighed. "I lost it while we were there. I must have dropped it in the water accidentally. I looked, but it had simply disappeared."

Margaret wasn't sure whether to feel disappointed or relieved. "I never saw anything like that," she lied. But in her mind she felt the rough texture of the baskets the rats wore to carry nuts and wild herbs back to the nest. When they swam in the creek, they often stacked the baskets just below the dried milkweeds on the bank there. That was all part of the secret. And this woman had held one of those baskets, had examined it while she stood on the beach where Margaret and Racso and Christopher played. Did she know other things about the valley? Did she have secrets, too?

The interview was over. Lindsey shook her hand warmly. She asked Margaret to call if she thought of anything she'd forgotten to say, and gave her the phone number. She walked with them across the parking lot beside the newspaper offices. It was dusk. The silhouettes of downtown buildings loomed to the west. The alley near their car was littered with trash and bits of brick. A gray, whiskered face looked up from its meal of garbage, then turned and fled.

"Christopher!" Arthur screamed. "Come back!"

The rat disappeared into a hole leading to the sewer.

Arthur saw the look on Margaret's face and realized his mistake. The rat in the alley had not been Christopher at all. He felt his heart break inside him, and he fell to the pavement, sobbing. "I told!" he cried.

His mother bent over him. "Artie," she whispered. "You spoke!" She picked him up and held him tightly in her arms.

Chapter 22

Justin wasn't that pleased that Racso and Christopher had spent all morning dreaming about their trip, instead of helping out. "Have you two forgotten that you're part of this community?" he asked sternly. "You were supposed to gather the rest of the carrots and onions. Instead you lay around chattering like a couple of squirrels."

"We weren't chattering. We were making plans."

"You can plan and work at the same time, can't you?"

Racso frowned. "*Last* fall Nicodemus said we could leave the carrots in the ground and put mulch over them. That was easier."

"Well, this year we're pulling the carrots up. And the onions, too!" Justin snapped. "Get to it!"

"I wish Nicodemus was back in charge," Racso muttered to Christopher. "I miss him." Racso hadn't meant for Justin to hear that, but he did. And instead of getting mad, he looked wistful.

"So do I." He took a deep breath. "But since he's not, we have to go on with our plans, and that means work. It seems hard now, but later you'll understand."

"These things are really big!" Racso was standing on his hind legs, his front paws curled around the green fronds of a carrot. He pulled with all his might, but the carrot didn't budge.

"Must be the new fertilizer Timothy suggested." Christopher pulled, too. "Arrrrrrrgh!"

"I've got an idea." Racso braced his hind paws against the carrot and leaned back, still holding on to the top. "Now you pull me."

"Okay." Christopher started out by putting his paws around Racso's middle, but he couldn't get a good grip, so he let go and grabbed his tail instead. "Heave-ho!"

"Ouch!"

"It's moving!"

"It isn't moving! I'm moving, because if I don't move you're going to pull my tail off!" Racso jumped off the carrot in disgust and rubbed his hindquarters where they attached to his tail. "That hurt!"

"Sorry." Christopher *did* seem sorry. "I was just trying to get the job done."

Racso kept rubbing.

"Margaret could have pulled these up in a minute," Christopher said. "And Artie could have carried them down to the nest in a big bundle." He sat down on the ground. "What do you think Artie's doing right now?"

"He's probably eating potato chips. That's what I'd be doing, if I were him."

"He's probably thinking about me, just like I'm thinking about him. He's wondering when I'll get there."

"He could be eating M & M's," Racso said. "Those are good, too."

"He and I swore an oath of friendship. We're going to be companions for the rest of our lives. We may not always be together . . . after all, friends have to part sometimes—like you and Timothy. But we'll always be thinking of each other."

"The first thing I'm going to do when we get to his house is look in the refrigerator," Racso said to himself.

"I heard that!" Christopher whirled around. "You're not even listening to me! You're thinking about food!"

"Oh!" Racso blinked. "I—"

"I thought you two were supposed to be pulling up carrots," Isabella said triumphantly. "But instead you're just standing here arguing."

"Where did *you* come from?"

"I was behind that bush counting turnips when I heard someone talking. Then the voices got so loud I couldn't concentrate. So I decided to investigate."

"You mean you were spying on us," Christopher said in disgust. "And now you're going to tattle to Justin."

"I have no need to tattle," Isabella said grandly. "Justin knows that *I'm* responsible. He's asked me to supervise the harvest of all the root crops. And that includes carrots."

"What?"

She nodded. "I've been named "Root Crop Coordinator.""

"Since when?"

"Since a half hour ago."

"Well, Justin talked to us since then, and he didn't mention you. Did he, Racso?"

Racso avoided answering deliberately. He didn't want to make Isabella mad. It was true that he and Christopher hadn't been working as hard as they should have. On the other hand, Isabella was acting stuck-up.

"We did try to pull the carrots up," he said. "But they won't come out. What's the hurry, anyway?"

"All I know is that all the root crops have to be harvested in the next two weeks," Isabella said. "Beatrice and Justin both said so. And I intend to make sure that happens."

"If you do, you might get promoted," Christopher said nastily, "to Cabbage Queen."

"You better pull up those carrots!"

"Leave me alone!" Christopher glared. "In two weeks I'll be on the way to see Artie. You won't be bossing me around then!"

"Artie, Artie, Artie! You're getting boring, Christopher."

"Come on, Isabella." Racso intervened. "You know you miss the children, too. You said so last night."

"Margaret, yes . . . she turned out to be a very nice girl, after I helped her move the nest. But Arthur flooded the storeroom, and he broke our bridge, too." Isabella's tone softened. She stopped. "Actually, I *do* miss him. He let me ride on his shoulder a couple of times, too. And Margaret used to sing a nice song to Artie when we were walking together at night. It was called, 'Twinkle, Twinkle, Little Star.'" Isabella sat down on the ground. "I wish I were going to see them," she sniffed. "I want to go, too."

Racso glanced at Christopher reassuringly, then turned to Isabella. "I'd love to have you come, but wouldn't someone else have to supervise the root crops? I mean, you'd have to give up your title, which would be too bad."

Isabella picked herself up off the ground and wiped her eyes.

"Of course *Sally* would do a good job supervising the root-crop harvest," Racso went on. "She's dependable, and she—"

"I *won't* go, even if you beg me," Isabella interrupted. "I'm needed here. I can't just run off and leave my work!"

Racso and Christopher didn't say anything.

"Now you two—get back to work!" Isabella commanded. And she marched off.

Chapter 23

After the interview Margaret couldn't stop worrying. When she got Artie alone, she gave him a tongue-lashing.

"There was only one thing we told you not to do," Margaret whispered fiercely. "One thing that could ruin everything."

Arthur kept his eyes on the floor.

"There are a million rats in the city," Margaret went on. "They live in the sewer systems, in the old buildings, in the trash. They don't have anything to do with rats like Christopher and Nicodemus."

Arthur's eyes filled with tears. You could have told me, he thought.

"We only asked you to keep one secret," Margaret said. "We thought you could do that much."

I *can* keep a secret, Arthur thought. He thought about the special place under the oak tree, and the secret in his closet. But of course he couldn't tell Margaret about that.

It was lonely, having a secret. As the days turned into weeks, Margaret wished she *could* be like Artie, who had blurted it out in one split second. But Artie was lucky—no one expected a little kid to make sense. She was different. She had to lie. And the worst part was lying to Leon.

She thought of Nicodemus and wondered where he was. He'd told her it would be hard, but she hadn't believed him. "I'll never tell," she'd shouted. But he hadn't expected that of her. "Do the best you can," he'd said.

Sometimes at night she talked to Artie about the rats. She'd sneak into his room when she was supposed to be doing her homework and sit down on the floor. "Remember the time when you and Christopher and I had the picnic in the garden?" she'd begin. Arthur would smile sleepily. "Remember the party after I moved the nest, when we all danced together? Remember the acorn bread Isabella made? Remember what it was like, sleeping in the hut at night?"

After she'd talked for a minute or two, Arthur

would be asleep. Sometimes she kept on talking anyway. It felt good to say the things she thought about out loud, even if he couldn't hear them. It was like sharing the secret. Sometimes she worried that Arthur would forget about the rats. Then she would really be alone.

"Do the best you can." Margaret thought about Nicodemus and marked off the days on her calendar. She had kept the secret two whole weeks; then, three. Sometimes she felt like a bomb about to explode. Other days she felt as fragile as a glass jar. If someone bumped her, she would break. Then the news would come trickling out for everyone to know.

One day when she was riding in the car with her mom she almost told. That morning her parents had given her a present: a Walkman. "I've noticed you've developed an interest in classical music," her mom said, smiling. Margaret blanched. She'd been turning on the radio at night because she felt too guilty sitting with her parents watching TV. They were so nice to her now: They couldn't stop asking, "Want some popcorn, Margaret?" "Is this the show you want to watch?" "How about a Coke?" The truth was she hadn't even noticed what station the radio was on.

They drove downtown to buy some tapes. On the way they passed the newspaper office.

"I've thought a lot about that evening when we met with the reporter," her mom said. "Arthur was more affected by the interview then he let on. He called that rat as if it were a pet." She glanced at Margaret. "You never talked about having a pet in the valley."

"We didn't. It was hard to find enough food for ourselves."

"I thought maybe there'd been a stray dog or cat, something like that."

"No." Margaret kept her eyes straight ahead.

"He was so distressed after he'd called to it. It was as if he'd done something terrible."

"Who knows? Artie's strange." Margaret tried to act bored, but a little voice inside her said, Lying again? She squirmed in her seat.

Her mom noticed that, because she said, "Don't worry about it, honey."

Margaret nodded. She tried to smile.

"Artie *is* sort of strange." Her mom smiled, too. "Just think, of all the animals to like . . ." She shuddered.

"Maybe rats aren't that bad," Margaret said weakly. "I think—"

"Oh, they are. They live off garbage, and they carry disease. In the Middle Ages they spread bubonic plague all through Europe."

"Oh." Margaret sat still, hating herself. She

couldn't even stick up for Nicodemus and Racso and Christopher, who had saved her life.

"Do the best you can." She marked another day off on the calendar. That was the day she'd found out her mom wouldn't want to know the truth, even if Margaret could tell her. Would it be the same with her dad? He asked more questions, but when he saw her getting upset, he'd always stop. "All that really counts is that you're okay," he'd say. He and her mom usually stuck together, almost as if they were one person instead of two. Margaret sighed. The secret hurt inside her, like a stomachache.

Leon was sitting in the middle of a pile of books and magazines, reading. At first he looked happy to see her, but then he seemed to remember that they weren't good friends anymore, and his eyes grew wary. Margaret smiled deliberately. "What are you doing?"

"Mom told me to sort this stuff out. It's my science fiction collection. And these science magazines came from Gram's. They were in her attic."

"I remember. We used to lie up there and look at the pictures."

"Right." Leon blinked.

"We had a lot of fun at her house."

"Yeah, she let us do anything! She understood us." Leon paused. His voice was low. "I used to think she'd live forever, like Gandalf. I thought she'd always be around when I needed her. And if it seemed like she wasn't, she'd show up anyway, just at the last moment. She'd tell me how to get out of danger. Or maybe she'd lead me into danger, but just enough so that I could get out of it myself." Leon held a book tight between his knees.

"You know what?" Margaret's voice trembled. "I knew somebody else like that."

"You did?"

She nodded. "He may be dead now. But he was wonderful."

"What was his name?"

"Nicodemus."

"I'll bet he's one of the ones you met this summer."

She nodded.

"I'll bet he was a wizard. And only kids could see him."

"I don't know about that. There weren't any grown-ups there—not human ones, anyway."

"He wasn't human?"

"No."

"What was he, then?"

Margaret felt the same dull pain in her stomach. "I'm not supposed to tell."

"Why not?"

"Like I said before, I have to protect them."

Leon stared. "They're aliens, aren't they? Like E.T."

"No." Margaret squirmed. "Leon, I'm not supposed to tell."

"But I'm just a kid. They like kids. They took care of you and Artie."

She nodded dumbly.

"I want to meet Nicodemus," Leon said. "If he's still alive, that is."

"You can't," Margaret said. She felt like crying.

"Why not?"

"He's gone away. There was something he had to do before he died."

"What?"

"I can't tell you anything else. Don't ask me, please."

"I want to know." Leon was staring at her.

"I can't tell you. I can't tell you anything else."

Chapter 24

It was Artie who noticed the calendar. He had snuck into Margaret's room while she was at school. He climbed up on the desk to reach the highest shelf of her bookcase, where she kept her baseball card collection. That was when he saw it. All the other days were marked over, with an "X"; but not this one. It had a bright-red circle around it.

He wanted to show her as soon as she got home from school; but Leon was there. So he kept coming into the bedroom and looking right at her, so she'd know there was something important. After a while she got annoyed.

"What is it, Artie? Why do you keep hanging around?"

He looked at her, then toward the desk. But it was Leon who saw the red circle.

"What's so important about today?"

"I don't know." Margaret came closer. "Did you do that, Artie? You know you're not supposed to touch my stuff . . ." Her voice died suddenly. She looked at Leon. "There's nothing at all important about today," she said. "It's just Artie, playing around with my Magic Markers. Next time I'm telling Mom," she added threateningly. "Now get out of here."

He went to his room smiling. He sat down to wait.

They came when he was supposed to be asleep. There was a tug on the blanket. Then a nose and whiskers appeared over the side of the bed.

"You're here!" Artie held Christopher tight. Racso stood nearby, grinning.

"Does Margaret know?"

Arthur nodded and pointed toward her bedroom.

"Go get her," Racso whispered. "But be quiet."

Margaret had to keep herself from running down the hall to Arthur's room. Once inside, she flung her arms around Racso. She wanted to tell him everything, but instead she just looked at him.

Racso stuck his chest out. "We arrived this morning. We snuck in quietly, but it turned out no one was home. We had some potato chips and a few malted milk balls, and I showed Christopher how to work the TV. Then we came upstairs and looked around."

"And circled the date on my calendar."

Racso laughed.

"I've thought of someplace wonderful to take you. We can go now, if you want," said Margaret.

"Maybe we should talk first." Christopher spoke up from Arthur's shoulder. "That's what Justin told us to do."

"Stop reminding me what Justin told us. I *know* what Justin told us."

"You don't act like you know."

"Shhhhh." Margaret tried to calm them down. "You'll wake up my parents. Anyway, I have to tell *you* something." She described what had happened in the parking lot.

"What did the reporter say afterward?"

"She asked me who Christopher was. I told her that Artie has imaginary friends, and that he used to talk to them in the valley. Then she asked why he'd say, 'I told,' and I said I didn't know."

"What was the reporter's name?"

"Lindsey something. Lindsey Scott, I think."

"Lindsey Scott! She's the one who came down our stream in a canoe. She found out that the man who was building the dam was a crook, and they stopped the project. She helped us."

"I remember her," Christopher said. "She was

wearing a green coat, and she had things in front of her eyes. Elvira said they were called glasses, and they were to help her see better."

"I'll tell Justin and Beatrice," Racso promised. "Is there anything else?"

Margaret hesitated. "Leon knows I didn't tell the whole truth. He knows Artie and I didn't survive on our own, that there was someone who helped us. But he doesn't know who. And he's only a kid, like me." She paused. "I almost told him," she admitted.

"But you didn't. That was good."

"I kept remembering what Nicodemus said: Do the best you can."

"I wonder where he is now. I wonder whether he got to the ocean." Racso sighed. "I miss him."

"So do I." Margaret couldn't keep the sadness out of her voice. She told them about Nicodemus leaving, just limping away into the brush without looking back. When she told about it, she began to cry.

"What's wrong?" Christopher's voice was gentle.

"Nobody knows you're real," Margaret sobbed. "Nobody but me. And Artie."

Later, when she felt better, Margaret tucked Racso and Christopher into her gym bag and took everyone on the subway. It was so late they were the only ones in the car. Arthur had pulled a heavy sweater over his pajamas. Margaret brought money and a package of peanut butter crackers, which they ate on the way. "This stop," she said. She led them partway down an alley beside a tall wire fence, and showed them a hole where the mesh had come unfastened from a metal post. Racso and Christopher darted through, and then Arthur crawled through on his hands and knees. Margaret slid through on her belly and took them to a round hut with flags on the top. She lifted Racso up so that he was looking into a face with evil eyes and flaring nostrils. He screamed.

"I'm sorry." She held him close. "I didn't know you'd think it was real. See—it's made of wood."

Racso stared. All around him were wooden faces. And beneath the faces were bodies: some with long skinny legs, some with humps, some with painted saddles.

"It's a merry-go-round," Margaret explained.

"A merry-go-round! Is this . . . ?"

"An amusement park! It's closed at night, so there's no guard. And Leon discovered the hole in the fence!"

Racso's heart swelled. "It's like a dream come true."

"I knew you'd love it." Margaret grinned. "So here we are!"

Christopher leaped from an elephant's trunk to

the back of a Bengal tiger. "Look at me, Artie," he shrieked. "I'm riding on a tiger! I'm taming a wild zebra! I'm floating on a swan!" He climbed into the central cylinder of the merry-go-round to see how it worked. In a minute they heard the tinkle of music, and the wooden stage lurched. Margaret boosted Arthur onto an ostrich. She rode a bear, and Racso rode in the pouch of a kangeroo. Then they switched around, and then they switched again. Christopher made the carousel speed up, and they clung tight to their animals. Then he made them go around backward.

"What next?" Racso jumped off a billy goat and landed running. "This way?"

"*This* way." Margaret pointed. "We can play the fishing game."

Margaret had chosen the fishing game because it was Arthur's favorite. She let him show the others what to do.

First he gave everyone a fishing rod. Then he let out his line until the hook floated among the little fish in a rubber tub. He caught one by its nose, reeled it in, and held it up for Margaret to read.

"Regular prize. That means you get one of these, Artie." She handed him a bottle of bubble soap. "You try it, Christopher."

The fishing pole was three times Christopher's

size, but he managed to reel in a fish. He read the tag on the bottom: Regular Prize. Next Margaret won a bottle of bubble soap. Then Racso threw his line in and swirled it around and around until he caught a bright-blue fish.

"Grand Prize!" Margaret was jealous. She'd always wanted to win the grand prize herself. She stood up on a chair and took down a gigantic stuffed cat. Racso and Christopher climbed its plush shoulders and stared into its marble eyes. They looked inside its ears and felt its long whiskers.

"I've never seen a cat before," Christopher whispered. "I want to take it home and put it on the playground!" Christopher stood up on the cat's head. "The other rats—"

"We can't take it," Racso interrupted. "These games cost money, and we haven't paid anything."

Christopher was crestfallen. "But we don't have any money!"

"I do." Margaret looked thoughtful. "But not a whole lot."

"We'd better put it back." Racso remembered what Beatrice had said: Don't steal anything. "Maybe Margaret can pay for one of the regular prizes."

And that was what they ended up doing. Then Arthur showed Racso and Christopher how to blow bubbles. Christopher held the wand in his tail and waved it back and forth over Racso's head, and Racso popped the bubbles with his nose. Then Margaret showed them how to blow slowly and steadily to make a really big bubble, and they let that one go, gliding high into the darkness.

"Hungry," Artie said softly.

"Me, too. I haven't had anything since those peanut butter crackers. But this is locked." Margaret pushed at the door of a wooden kiosk.

"I think I can crawl in the vent." Racso pointed out a metal cylinder at the top of the booth. Margaret lifted him up, and he scrambled through and down the window to the door, where he slid the bolt back.

"Let's see what's on the menu: hot dogs, hamburgers, cotton candy, pizza, milkshakes, french fries, soda, candy bars . . . I'll have one! One of each!" Racso grinned.

"Me, too . . . How about you, Artie?"

"Pizza!"

"Margaret?"

She put some money on the counter. "I'll have an extra-large grape soda, french fries, and a cheeseburger."

They took turns playing host. Margaret figured out how to work the griddle while Arthur shaped the hamburgers. Christopher filled a cone with pink cotton candy. Racso threw french fries one by one

[219]

into the fryer. Margaret slid a frozen pizza into the oven. "Din-nuh at eight," she announced, bowing low to her company. "Din-nuh at nine!" Racso swept off his beret and graciously kissed Christopher on the paw. "Din-nuh at ten!" Christopher planted a kiss on Arthur's nose. Arthur giggled.

They spread the feast on the floor and helped themselves. Arthur showed them how to dip french fries in ketchup, and helped Christopher clean wads of cotton candy off his whiskers. Racso's stomach bulged from candy and milkshakes and pizza. Margaret had polished off her soda and most of her cheeseburger and was lying on the floor with her chin between her hands. That was when the thought hit her.

"When will you come back?"

"I . . . I don't know. We didn't talk to Justin and Beatrice about that."

"I want you to. You're my best friends now—you and Nicodemus. And he's gone."

They were quiet. Sadness fell over the group. It could be months—even a year—before they saw each other again. Racso tried to break the mood.

"Wait till the rats at home hear about this meal! They'll be so jealous!"

"They're probably eating acorn bread and carrot sticks right now." Even Margaret had to smile at the comparison. "Rat food isn't my idea of great eating, that's for sure."

"If only we had a way to remember tonight. . . ."

"There is a way!" Margaret was on her feet. "Quick. Let's clean this place up, and then I'll show you."

The others didn't recognize the metal stall with pictures stuck on the sides and a sign that said: Four for a dollar. Margaret had to explain it.

"We put the money in the slot and jump inside. There's a camera hidden behind that wall, and it'll take our pictures."

Margaret settled Arthur on the seat with Christopher and Racso in his arms. She stuck the dollar in and got in herself. Flash! That was one picture. She grinned and moved closer to Artie and the rats. Flash! There was another. They waved hands and paws for the third. Then Artie shouted, "Me and Christopher!" so Margaret and Racso ducked outside.

Waiting for the pictures seemed to take forever, but when they slid out the little slot they were perfect! Here was Racso, his beret cocked at just the right angle, his face peering out beside Margaret's chin. Arthur and Christopher looked as if they belonged together. And there was a picture for each of them!

"Wait till the others see this!" Racso waved his in the air, as if he were already showing it off to the rats in the valley.

Margaret didn't say anything, but she wrapped

the photo lovingly in a Kleenex and put it in her gym bag. "We'd better head for home," she said softly. "Artie will fall asleep on his feet if we don't leave soon."

They were headed back to the hole in the fence when Christopher noticed the set of keys hanging from the starter of the Tilt-a-Whirl.

"Someone must have left them there by accident," Margaret said.

"It's just asking for us to ride it. Please?"

"I guess one ride wouldn't hurt anything," Margaret said.

In fact they rode on the Tilt-a-Whirl five times. The first time Christopher was so scared he really didn't enjoy it. The second time they enjoyed it so much they thought they'd better do it once more. The third time Arthur threw up. The fourth time they gave themselves a treat after cleaning up the mess that Arthur had made; but he sat on the bench outside, looking sad. The fifth time they rode it together one last time. By the time they crawled through the fence it was very late; and when they got to the subway stop a metal grate had been pulled across the entrance.

"We'll have to take a taxi," Margaret said. "I've got a couple more dollars in my pocket."

She tucked the rats into the gym bag. Luckily a cab came around the corner just then. Margaret helped Arthur into the backseat and put the bag in between them.

"Out late for your age, aren't you?" The driver was a black man with a kindly face. He looked concerned.

"Yes." Margaret thought fast. "Family emergency, you see."

"Emergency?"

"My mom had a baby."

"Oooooh." The driver's face brightened. "Boy or girl?"

"Girl. Her name's Edna."

"Congratulations."

"Thanks."

"What does the little fellow think of her?"

"Oh, Artie? He thinks she's adorable."

"Great." The cab driver seemed genuinely happy for them. "Makes for a nice family, when nobody's jealous."

"This is our house." Margaret gave the driver the rest of her money, which included a thirty-five-cent tip. She led Arthur around to the back door. It was unlocked, as they had left it. They crept upstairs, pausing at the door of her parents' bedroom. Snores. She helped Arthur pull off his sweater. She made Racso a nest at the foot of her mattress. Then she put on her nightgown and settled into bed.

"This was one of the best nights in my whole

life," she whispered. "Good night." She switched off the light on the bedside table.

Arthur and Christopher stayed up. Arthur showed the rat his favorite toys and books. Then he took him into the back of his closet, under the eaves. It was time to show Christopher the secret.

At first Christopher didn't know what to say. Then he remembered how, when he was very small, he used to make marks in the sand beside the creek with a sharp stick. He'd pretended he was making lists, the way his own father listed the bins of grain and vegetables for Nicodemus each fall.

"It's writing, isn't it?" he asked softly.

Arthur nodded solemnly. Behind him the wall was covered with marks: loops and squiggles, straight and crooked lines. There was a mark for everything that had ever happened to Arthur, the good things and the bad ones, too. "I did it all by myself," he said.

He showed Christopher the part about being a baby, and getting sick, and going to the hospital for shots. He showed him where he and Margaret got lost and found the valley, and met the rats. Beyond that the wall was blank.

There was a small window at the back of the eaves, and on the windowsill was a black crayon. Arthur picked it up and made a mark on the wall.

"That's about our visit, isn't it?"

Arthur nodded. He'd known Christopher would understand.

"And the blank space is for all the other things that will happen to us. Remember the Brave Explorers Club? Well, the meeting we'll have tonight won't be the last one. I don't plan to stay in Thorn Valley all my life. When I'm grown up I'm going to travel all round the world. You can come with me, Artie." Christopher's voice had grown hushed. "We'll go by bus, and train, and car, and when we come to the ocean we'll get on a boat and sail to new places. We'll see everything there is to see: animals and people and plants and mountains and deserts. You'll be able to talk then, and we'll talk, and we'll write down our adventures, just the way you have here."

Arthur nodded.

"The Brave Explorers will hold their next meeting right now," Christopher said. "Let it come to order, please."

It was late when Arthur went to bed. He knew Christopher would leave before he woke up. He hugged his friend and kissed the top of his furry head. They looked out the window at the gray dawn to the east. In the dim light they didn't see the figure behind the lamppost, watching them.

Chapter 25

Lindsey Scott couldn't get the incident in the parking lot out of her mind. She described it to her boss, Dave Castle, while he leaned back in his chair, puffing on a cigar. Dave was cynical: "The kids cooked up a plan to get a little more attention, Lindsey. Forget about it."

But she couldn't forget about it. For one thing, there was the way the girl had answered the questions, as if she'd figured out each answer ahead of time. And the boy had cried, "I told." But what had he told?

And there was the rat. There were thousands of them in the city, and that one hadn't seemed any different from the rest. But the spring the dam was being built in Thorn Valley there'd been talk of rats, too; so much talk that Lindsey had finally written an article about all the rumors. Now she typed something into her computer. It purred and spat out a length of paper.

RUMOR TIES RATS TO DAM PROBLEMS
by Lindsey Scott

Interviews with workmen at the site of the now-defunct Thorn Valley Dam suggest a curious culprit for the continuing problems there: rodents.

Two night watchmen assigned to the dam's computer headquarters described finding two rats there, and in separate interviews agree that one of them, described as short and wearing a small black hat, had written the word "stop" on a piece of paper in the office.

Another construction worker described finding the body of a charred rodent adjacent to a severed electric line. The resulting blackout kept the dam from opening as scheduled.

Still another worker said he saw rodentlike tracks on the floor near the emergency generators, which also failed the day the dam was scheduled to open. . . .

Lindsey put the paper on her desk and stood up. Outside the office window the branches of a small tree broke the sky behind it into fragments . . . the pieces of a puzzle. If you moved to a different spot, the sky would be whole again, the puzzle complete. The interviews at the dam site, the girl's story, the rat in the alley, Arthur's "I told": these were also pieces in a puzzle. Lindsey rearranged them in her mind, thinking, Where do I go from here?

"You're crazy," Dave said, when she told him what she was thinking about. But it was he who suggested the phone calls. "Rats are thieves," he said. "If there are rats near the valley, the farmers are probably being robbed blind. Call them up and ask them."

She almost gave up. She had to get maps and then call the state tax office to find out who owned the land around there. Looking at the map, she thought the valley seemed so remote that nothing there would affect farmers on the other side of the mountains. But it was an idea, and right now it was the only idea she had. She picked up the phone.

Four calls later, she was more discouraged than ever. All the farms had rats, and if she thought there was something unusual about them, she must have been watching too much Walt Disney. One farmer had hung up in disgust.

There was one number left. The name beside it seemed familiar: Paul Fitzgibbon. But it was his wife who answered the phone.

"Rats?" she said. "Oh, yes, we've had a lot of rats; rats and mice. But anywhere you have corn and silage, you're going to have rats."

Anything peculiar? Not really, not that she could rightly recall. Of course the whole thing with the children coming back the way they did, that had been strange, but she counted it a miracle. She was a believer. There had been other times when they themselves had been blessed: When the dam got closed down, for instance. Why, they would have had to sell their land, even though it had been in the family for three generations.

"About the *rats*," Lindsey repeated. "Has there been anything peculiar about the rats?"

"Oh, the rats." Mrs. Fitzgibbon paused. "Like I told you, we have 'em, but there's nothing *special* about them. We know that, because one day a couple of years ago some scientists came out here and tried to trap some of the big ones that lived under my rosebush. There was something particular they were looking for, but they never told us what. But the nest was full of garbage, and all the rats got away but one. They were awful disappointed."

"The one they did get," Lindsey asked, "was there anything unusual about it?"

"They never told us," Mrs. Fitzgibbon said. "But when they saw the nest all full of rotten food they shook their heads. 'They wouldn't be living that way, not now,' one of them said. 'Not if it was *them*.' "

"I wonder what they meant by that."

The woman's voice over the phone was puzzled, too. "They didn't say. In fact they were right secretive about what they were looking for."

"Do you remember their names?"

"No, I sure don't. But they were from some big laboratory—government owned, I believe. It had letters for its name." She thought aloud. "What was it, now? N . . . I . . . something . . ."

"N.I.H.?" Lindsey caught her breath. She had a feeling that a piece of the puzzle was about to slide into place. "That would be the National Institute of Health. . . ."

"It wasn't that." Mrs. Fitzgibbon sounded certain. "There were four letters, as I recall. N . . . I . . . *M* . . . H, I believe it was. NIMH. It's been a few years, so I'm surprised I can recollect it. But I'll never forget how disappointed they were when they saw that garbage. I don't know what they expected, but it wasn't that."

"The guy at NIMH was really excited that I called," Lindsey told Dave in the lunchroom. "He wanted to come down and talk to the kids right away."

"You're kidding."

She shook her head. "He said, 'You don't understand what it would mean to find those animals. The discovery would shock the scientific world.'"

"So when's he coming?"

"Oh." Lindsey seemed a little embarrassed. "He isn't. I told him not to."

"Why not?"

"Because we don't have any facts."

"But suppose it is true." Dave wrinkled his heavy brows. "Suppose it's true, and he goes to another paper with the information, and they print it first."

Lindsey shrugged. "I'm not going to write an article unless I know what it says is true."

"You ought to lean on those kids. Question them again."

"I'm thinking about calling up the girl, Margaret. But I have to figure out exactly what to ask first. I don't want to pressure her."

"Let the scientist question her," Dave said. "What's his name?"

"Dr. Schultz." Lindsey finished her coffee and pushed herself back from the table. "We could end up looking pretty foolish if we're not careful about this. I don't plan to move too fast."

"Just don't let another paper get it first, that's all I'm saying. If there's something to it, we ought to publish it first."

Chapter 26

After Christopher left, Arthur felt sad. But he felt something else, too. He got up late and put his pants and shirt on all by himself. He poured a bowl of cereal and only spilled a little bit. When his mom came into the kitchen, he was sitting at the counter eating.

"Why, Artie, you're all dressed. And you got your own breakfast. I didn't know you were big enough to do that!" She smiled.

He smiled back and said, "Yes." She had noticed it, too. He was bigger.

Things were different at nursery school. Arthur couldn't stop thinking about what Christopher had said: They would travel around the world and write down their adventures. Arthur stood up tall and looked around the room.

Teresa was at the snack table, pouring juice. Some of the children were playing with clay, and some were gluing colored paper on cloth. Stevie was playing with the yellow truck, pushing it around in circles. The truck made a high whining sound, as if it were real. Arthur swallowed. His hands clenched and opened. He went over to Stevie and shouted, "I WANT THAT TRUCK!" Everyone turned and stared.

"No," Stevie said. "Anyway, you can't talk."

"I CAN TOO!"

"Well, it's my turn now."

Teresa was watching from the table. "I think it *is* Arthur's turn," she said calmly. "And he did ask for it." She smiled at Arthur, a great big smile.

"Oh, all right," Stevie handed over the truck. "But I want it next."

Arthur got down on his hands and knees. He'd asked for the truck, and now he had it! Christopher would be proud of him! He pushed the truck in circles, saying, "Vroooooom, vroooom, vroooom."

Margaret faked it that day. She told her mom she had a headache, and she slept all morning. When she got up and went down to the kitchen, there was a note on the table.

Gone to take Artie to school, then to work. Hope
you feel better.

Love, Mom.

Margaret made herself a peanut butter and jelly
sandwich and was starting to pour a glass of Pepsi
when the back door opened.

"Leon! How come you're not at school?"

"When I found out you weren't there, I left."

"How come?"

Leon leaned forward, so that his heavy glasses
were only a few inches from Margaret's nose. "*I
know.*"

"You know what?"

"I know about *them.*"

"No, you don't! I mean . . ." Margaret dropped
the can of Pepsi and it rolled across the floor, spouting
brown liquid. "Damn!" She grabbed a paper towel
and began to clean up the mess, as if everything
were normal. She tried to keep her voice steady.
"What are you talking about?"

"The rats. I saw them last night with my binocu-
lars. I was spying on you, because I wanted to know
the truth."

"Oh." Margaret stood up slowly. She didn't know
what to say.

"I saw that they can talk. One of them was talking
to Artie. And one of them was wearing a little hat."

"Racso," Margaret murmured.

[234]

"That's why your calendar was circled—they were coming to visit. And they took you someplace last night. You're under their power. But I'm going to help you break free."

"Wait a minute—"

"I've got it all figured out, so you don't need to deny it, Margaret. They *are* aliens, and they landed in the valley because it's so remote. They took the form of rats thinking that people would leave them alone. But rats are everywhere, on farms and in the cities. That meant they could learn about different ways people live. . . ."

"NO!" Margaret had to shout to make him stop. "You've got it all wrong, Leon. If you'll be quiet for a minute, I'll tell you the truth."

"How will I know it's really the truth? Last time you—"

"Just shut up and listen!"

Leon smiled a little smile and shrugged his shoulders. "For once you sound like your old self. Okay, shoot."

"First of all, they're not from outer space. They escaped from a laboratory where they'd been given shots as part of an experiment. The shots were supposed to make them really smart, and they worked. They worked so well that Justin and Nicodemus figured out how to get out of the cages, and they all escaped from NIMH."

"NIMH? That's the National Institute of—"

"Right. You know I wouldn't have heard of it if they hadn't told me. Anyway, they ended up living on a farm. Later they decided to move to the valley and become more self-sufficient. They wouldn't have to worry about being caught there, either."

Leon was staring at her. "I've read about experiments like that," he said slowly. "In an old *Science Digest* from Gram's there was an article about a guy who—" He stopped short, as if he'd thought of something more important. "Where are they? I want to talk to them."

"You can't."

"I've got to. You should have introduced me when they first came. You know I'm planning to be a scientist when I grow up."

"They're already gone. I took them to the amusement park last night, and they left early this morning. All I have left is their picture."

"Let me see it." Leon's tone was demanding, and he looked upset.

"Here." She produced the little square from the pocket of her pajamas. "That's Racso, with the hat, and this is Christopher. He's crazy about Artie."

Leon looked at the picture only long enough to make sure it was real. Then he headed for the door. "Which way did they go? I want to catch up with them. Whoever discovers them will be famous."

"You don't understand, Leon. They saved my life. They're my friends."

"Yeah. And I used to be your friend, until you met them. And then I wasn't important anymore—not like them—or Elinor."

"Leon, please. I wanted to tell you more than anything. I wanted to sit with you, but I was afraid you'd figure it out. I don't even like Elinor!"

"I'm going to find them, even if I have to ride my bike all the way to the valley."

"You can't do that. Please!"

Her voice rose in a wail.

But Leon went out the door without looking back.

Chapter 27

Lindsey Scott heard the phone ring just as she was leaving to go to lunch. She went back into her office and picked it up. The voice at the other end of the line was strange.

"Who? Margaret? Margaret Livingstone? . . . Yes, I remember you . . ."

"You gave me your phone number the night you interviewed me." Margaret had to choke back tears. "You said if I wanted to talk to you more . . ."

"I remember."

"I need your help. I know this sounds crazy, but you've been to the valley yourself. I need you to take me there."

"But the last road is miles away from—" Lindsey stopped herself. "Why?"

"I have a friend who's on his way there now, and I have to catch up with him. It's urgent. If I don't stop him, something terrible could happen."

"Do your parents know about this?"

"There's not time to tell them, not right now. I'm not sure they even want to know the truth."

"The truth?" Lindsey paused. "Does the truth have anything to do with rats?"

There was a silence on the other end of the phone.

"Hello? Margaret?"

"Yes," said the girl in a faint voice. "It does."

Margaret was waiting in front of the house when Lindsey pulled up. She was wearing jeans and a sweatshirt, and her hair looked uncombed. She jumped into the front seat and slammed the door.

"Who is it we're looking for?"

"My friend Leon. He's a skinny black kid with glasses, and he's riding a red ten-speed."

"Which way did he go?"

"That way." Margaret pointed. "He left a half hour ago."

"It's a long way to the valley—hours and hours."

"Please hurry. We have to find him."

"Okay. We'll head out Route Fifteen. But while I'm driving, I want you to tell me what's going on."

The story was so incredible that Lindsey would never have believed it if it hadn't fit so perfectly with the other pieces of the puzzle. The girl even knew Dr. Schultz's name. And she was a different child from the one Lindsey had met on the night of the interview: frightened and intense. Her face was pressed against the car window: "Where could he be?"

"I don't know. I don't think he could have got farther than this in a half hour."

"Could he have gone another way?"

Lindsey frowned. "I don't think so. This is the only road that heads toward the valley. But he may not have known that. Or maybe . . ." she paused. "Maybe he was just trying to scare you. Maybe he really didn't plan to go there at all."

"I saw him get on his bike, and he was wearing a knapsack."

"Let's turn around and look again. We must have missed him."

They drove back slowly, checking both sides of the road, but there was no sign of Leon. They even stopped in front of his garage, to see if he had come back. But the door was open, and his bike was still gone.

"I've got to find him." Margaret twisted her hands

in front of her. "I hurt his feelings by lying to him, and now he's really mad."

"You lied about the valley?"

She nodded. "I'd promised them I would. They're afraid if Dr. Schultz finds out about them, he'll put them back in the laboratory. For them, that's death."

"What if someone else went in his place, just to talk with them?"

"I guess that would be okay." Margaret looked as if she were about to cry. Lindsey put one arm around her. "We'll find him."

They drove out Route 15 again, this time stopping to ask at gas stations. No one had seen a black boy on a red bicycle. Margaret was ready to give up when she thought of something.

"I know this sounds crazy, but I thought of another place we could look."

"Where?"

"It's downtown, next to an office building. 1362 Reed Street."

"What makes you think Leon might be there?"

"It's a long story. . . ." Margaret's voice trembled. "You see, his grandma used to live there, and we used to visit her, but this summer while I was away, she died. She loved Leon a lot and he loved her, too. He left so upset, I thought that maybe if he did change his mind about going to the valley, he might . . ."

"It's worth a try." Lindsey turned the car toward downtown.

They didn't talk on the way there, but when they reached the high rise Margaret showed Lindsey how to drive around back and up the alley. There, next to the towering brick building, was a tiny wooden house. It was surrounded by a tall chain-link fence, and leaning against the fence was a red bicycle.

Margaret jumped out and motioned for Lindsey to stay put. She climbed the fence in long, easy strides, swung over the top, and dropped. The back door was locked, but a window on the side was partly opened. She climbed through.

"Leon?"

There was no answer. The familiar walls looked down at her: pictures of Leon as a baby, a toddler, Leon sitting in front of a birthday cake, Leon holding a bunch of red balloons, Leon holding a trophy from the science fair. The yellow cloth on the kitchen table was dusty, and the coal stove wasn't polished the way it used to be. "Leon?" she called. Her voice echoed through the empty rooms.

He had to be here. She poked her head into each room, climbed the stairs and checked there, too. Finally she went up the worn steps to the attic.

He was facing the door when she came in. He looked scared.

[242]

"Did you change your mind about going to the valley?"

He nodded. "It was too far. Anyway, I didn't want you to end up hating me."

"I'm sorry I lied. I'm sorry about everything."

Leon looked at the floor. "I had a terrible summer," he said in a high, choked voice. "First Gram died, and then you died, too. When it turned out you weren't dead I was so happy. But when you came back you were different."

"But that's over, and now you know the truth." Margaret swallowed. "You can cry if you want to," she said softly. "I did, when Nicodemus left, and lots of other times, too."

"No." But a tear ran down Leon's cheek. He wiped it away with his fist.

"I'm going to take you there sometime, Leon—I promise. You'll like them a lot. They've got their own world there, with crops and schools and doctors and everything. They'll like you, too. I know because I already told them about you. I even told them about this house."

"You did?"

"Yep. I told them about the stuff we used to do here in the summer, like flying paper planes from the roof, and what your gram said to the people who complained."

"What did they say?"

"They said we were lucky."

They were silent for a moment. Then Margaret said, "I really did want to tell you right from the moment I got back. Having to keep it to myself was awful. I was going to tell my mom, but I found out she hates rats, so I couldn't. Then you figured it out. I was so worried about your going to the valley that I called Lindsey. It turned out she'd almost figured it out, too."

"Who's Lindsey?"

"She's a reporter, and she's been to the valley before to write about it. She was helping me look for you. She's outside in her car."

"She's outside?"

Margaret nodded.

"Does she know the part about NIMH?"

"Yeah. She'd even talked to the guy who did the experiment. His name is Dr. Schultz."

"Is she going to tell him?"

"I . . . I don't think so. She's nice. But I have to talk to her more about that."

"You'd better. Reporters usually write articles about whatever they find out."

They walked together down the two flights of stairs to the kitchen. Margaret stopped there, remembering the afternoon meals of coconut cake and lemonade Leon's grandmother had made for them. He wasn't the only one who missed her. She told him so, and he nodded. He put out one hand with the palm up. "Friends?"

She slapped it, hard. "Friends!"

They climbed out the window, pulled it shut, and climbed over the fence. Lindsey put her head out the car window.

"Everything okay?"

"Yep." Margaret smiled.

"You must be Leon."

"I am."

Together they fitted the bike in the trunk and got into the front seat. On the way home they talked about the valley. Margaret didn't try to hide anything. She told about Nicodemus and Racso and Christopher and Justin and Beatrice and Isabella. She talked about the hawk's nest and the gardens and the wheatfield. She talked so much she thought she would run out of words, but there were always more things to tell, things that had been bottled up inside her for weeks.

And Lindsey listened. Even when her thoughts had strayed to the unbelievable, she hadn't imagined the story Margaret was telling now. She wanted to question every word; but she also just wanted to listen.

Margaret told about the visit. She told about the amusement park, and the merry-go-round, and the Tilt-a-Whirl, and the photo booth. She started to tell about their supper when Lindsey interrupted her.

"You have a picture of you and the rats?"

"Yes. It's at home in the pocket of my pajamas. I showed it to you, didn't I, Leon?"

"I'd like to see that picture," Lindsey said. She added, "Remember when we were looking for Leon on the road? And you told me that the rats were afraid of Dr. Schultz, because they thought he would put them back in the laboratory?"

Margaret nodded.

"What if someone went in his place, just to talk to them?"

Margaret didn't say anything.

"Well?"

"I think . . . it would be okay. If the person were nice, and promised not to hurt them or tell where they lived."

"What if you went with me? If it were okay with your parents, that is."

"Me, too," Leon said. "Don't forget about me."

"Him, too."

Margaret nodded. But she wondered what her parents would say when they knew the truth. And the rats: would they welcome Leon and Lindsey to the valley? The valley. The thought of being there again filled her with joy.

Chapter 28

The person Margaret worried most about after she'd told the secret was Artie. She wondered if he'd understand, or if he'd just think she was terrible. How she'd scolded him the night he'd shouted at the rat in the alley! If only she could take back the things she'd said! She went upstairs to talk to him.

"You see, Artie, Leon figured it out. And he was going there by himself. So I called Lindsey for help. I didn't mean to tell her; I just wanted to find Leon. But it turned out she asked about them. And when we were together, the truth came pouring out."

She looked at Artie. He was sitting in his little rocking chair, looking at his sneakers. She went on nervously:

"Lindsey's nice. She wants to go to the valley, and she wants you and me and Leon to go with her. She won't hurt the rats, or tell where they live."

Artie didn't say anything.

"I wish I hadn't told her. But I didn't know what else to do." Margaret swallowed.

Arthur looked up and saw that Margaret was afraid. Until this summer he hadn't even known that she cared about him. And now she was afraid. "It's okay," he said softly.

Lindsey told Margaret's parents. Margaret didn't want to go into the living room where they were talking. When they came out, her mom and dad looked at her as if they weren't sure what to think. Lindsey arranged for Margaret's dad to come with them to the valley. He hugged her and said, "Your mom and I have agreed that what happened while you were gone isn't the most important thing to us. The important thing is that you're here."

Margaret felt a little hurt by the doubt in his voice. "Wait till you see the valley, Dad. You'll love it. And the rats . . ."

Her mom put one hand to her mouth. "Oh, Margaret," she said.

They boarded a helicopter on a Saturday morning in early spring: Margaret, Arthur, and their dad; Leon, Lindsey—and Dave Castle, her editor, with a camera around his neck. Lindsey hadn't wanted Dave to come, but he was set on having pictures, although he'd promised not to reveal where the rats lived. They had had to wait until spring because it was impossible to land in the valley during the winter.

Margaret squirmed in her seat. She couldn't help thinking that the trip was a mistake. Now they were rising above the city. The streets and buildings looked like the little pieces in a board game. Leon pointed.

"There's the stadium! And there's the zoo!" He grinned, his face bright with excitement. Margaret smiled back, but a little voice in her head said, What if the rats aren't glad to see us?

"Look, Artie." Leon gestured out the window. "There's a school—see the track? And that's a farm. Remember what cows say?"

"Moooo," Artie said abruptly. He didn't feel like talking. He wondered when they would get to the valley. He wondered if Christopher knew he was coming. Christopher would like the helicopter.

"Look!" Leon pointed up ahead. "That's the state forest. See all the trees? And you can see the mountains just beyond."

Sure enough, Margaret could see the contours of the land rising. Outcroppings of rock dotted the ridges. The forest was green and brown, covered with tiny bare sticks that were really the trunks of trees far below.

"There's snow on some of the mountains! Look! There—and there!"

Now even Arthur was straining to see. Margaret wondered which cliff she'd climbed to get the hawk's nest. She looked for the mouth of the cave where they'd met Christopher. But from so high up, the mountains all looked alike.

The helicopter hovered over the ridge, then flew across. Margaret wondered if the rats had seen it yet. Below were the sides of the mountains, rock-strewn and brown; beyond them was the floor of the valley. Lindsey had said they would land in the meadow north of Emerald Pond and walk along the creek. Margaret had tried to draw a map showing how to get to the nest, but it was hard to remember how the creek curved.

"Look! There's the meadow!" Margaret was excited despite herself. She felt like shouting to the rats, "It's us, Margaret and Artie!" She punched Leon on the arm, and he grinned.

"We're coming down," the pilot said. "Make sure your seat belts are fastened tight."

The helicopter touched ground, jolted, and was still. Outside the window was a field covered with brown grass, and above it a brilliant blue sky. The passengers stood up. Margaret realized that everyone was nervous. The pilot unbolted the door and lowered a set of black steps to the ground.

"Why don't you go first?" Lindsey suggested. "That way, if they're watching, they'll know who we are."

"They'll be watching. They have a sentry tower beyond the garden."

She went down the steps. The cold air hit her first, and she gasped. It was still winter here. She gazed over the landscape: there, to her left, were the mountains that stood between the valley and the state forest; beneath them, clumps of green, were the pines and cedars; then the mixed brown of thickets, the bare tree trunks, the meadow grass. To the right and ahead the silhouette of the stream curved in a thick, wavy line. The pond was hidden by a dip in the ground. She'd thought the top of the tower would be visible from here, but she couldn't see it. She took a few steps, a lump in her throat.

Then the others were down, too. Lindsey blinked: She had forgotten the stark beauty of the valley, framed by dark mountains on both sides. Arthur had that blank look that meant Don't speak to me. Leon was like a burr at Margaret's side, asking questions. The others were quiet.

"We go this way to get to the nest." Margaret

gestured in the direction of the stream. "Once we cross it—over by that walnut tree there are stepping stones—we'll be able to see Emerald Pond. The gardens are just beyond it."

They walked single file, the frosty grass dampening their shoes. Deer tracks were frozen in the winter mud, and raccoons had left their handprints along the shore of the creek. The stepping stones were there, just as Margaret had remembered.

"There!" The pond lay before them, green and glassy, like a bright eye. There was ice around the edges. "But the diving platform is gone!" Margaret couldn't hide her disappointment. Had they taken it down for the winter? She led the others around to the right. There she saw something even stranger: The dam, which she had helped build, had disappeared. She ran along the bank, looking. Here was the exact spot where they had built it, with the sandbank to one side and the rocky shelf on the other. But the stones were gone, gone from the water, not even tumbled up on the bank where ice had dislodged them. She stared.

"What is it?" Leon asked quickly. She shook her head: She couldn't answer, not yet.

She hurried on, not waiting for the others. She came to the edge of the gardens. The carefully manicured plots of cabbages, beets, onions, and carrots were gone; there was only dirt, with a few stones in it. There were no beehives, and where Margaret remembered a row of blackberry bushes, only one scraggly plant remained. There was no sign the rats had ever lived here, only the brown meadow grass, the mud, here and there a bedraggled clump of vines.

"It was here," Margaret whispered.

"What?"

"Their garden!" She moved her arm in a circle in front of them. "The broccoli was over there—I remember because Artie stepped on it by accident. And the potatoes were here, and the cabbages right there, and the water pipe came up just about there— that was for the hot months, in case there wasn't enough rain. And the bamboo they made the pipes out of grew there—" She held her arm still, then let it drop.

Leon looked at her doubtfully. "Are you sure we're in the right spot?"

She nodded. "The nest is on the other side of that grove of pines. It was, at least."

He glanced over one shoulder. "Here come the others."

She had almost forgotten about them. She didn't want to see them now. She turned and ran, Leon beside her. "Come on!"

She ran through the pine grove, slowing down enough to notice that the clearing contained a massive bramble. The paved walk that led to the grove was gone. She found the clay bank where the nest had been. The doors and windows were smoothed out. Even the little bamboo faucet that had gotten Arthur into so much trouble was gone.

Margaret was flooded with disappointment. The valley had changed. "Where are they?" she whispered.

"I think they ran away," Leon said.

"But why?"

"They were afraid—afraid of being caught."

"I would never hurt them—never!"

"You wouldn't—they know that. And I wouldn't. We're just kids. But the others—"

"Lindsey's nice!"

"But her boss? Or the pilot?" Leon shrugged. "They couldn't be sure who would come."

"Margaret?" Her dad was standing with Lindsey and Dave beside the pine grove. She walked back slowly. "They're not here," she said.

Lindsey took a step toward her, as if she wanted to help. "But what about the gardens? And the nest? And the other places you told me about?"

"It's all changed. The gardens were right over there."

Dave walked over to where the lettuce and spinach should be. "It's full of rocks," he said. He picked some up and showed them.

"Honey, are you sure we're in the right place?" Her dad put his hands on her shoulders. Staring

[254]

into the blue wool of his jacket, Margaret remembered the rows of beets and onions and lettuces
laid out so neatly in the dark, crumbling earth. Yet
here there were only mud and stones and brambles.

"I don't know," she murmured. "I just don't
know."

She showed them the other places: the nest, the
wheatfield, the dam. They were all changed, or
gone. She felt as if she were in a dream, except
that it was real, and now. And suddenly the summer
seemed unreal, as if it had never happened at all.

"But you have the picture," Lindsey said gently.
"Remember? The one you took at the amusement
park?"

"The picture." Margaret nodded dumbly. The
others were standing around her in a circle. She
wanted to run away, but she couldn't. Then suddenly she felt what it must be like to be trapped
once and for all. Inside a cage you wouldn't see
the sun or moon, feel the earth under your feet,
feel the rain or wind or dew. Of course they had
run away. And she would do nothing else that would
let them be found.

"The picture," Margaret repeated. "It wasn't
real."

Lindsey looked at her oddly, as if she sensed the
change. "Leon saw it, too. It was in the pocket of
your pajamas."

"No."

Lindsey looked at Leon. He looked down at the ground, and then he looked at Margaret. "I never saw it," he said.

They stood together silently. Dave put the camera in his coat pocket. Then her dad stepped out of the circle and hugged her tight. "It's okay, honey," he said.

They left the valley an hour later. Margaret didn't want to go. She was held by memories: sunny days, hard work, the smell of pine needles, the taste of creek water, the feel of rock under her hands and knees. She had come from one world into another: rising from an armchair in front of the television to pass through a door into a life she couldn't have imagined. The rats had been part of that, of course. But even if she never saw them again—she closed her eyes tight when she thought of that—even if she didn't, she had learned from the valley itself.

Leon sat beside her on the ride home. When their eyes met, Margaret put one finger to her lips. "Later," she murmured. He nodded slightly.

The helicopter brought them back over the mountains and forest, over the green pastures to the suburbs and into the city itself. Like a metal bug it hovered over factories and skyscrapers, schools and offices. Before they landed, Lindsey put one hand on Margaret's shoulder.

"You have my phone number," she said softly.

Margaret nodded. She kept her eyes straight ahead.

A moment later they got off. Her mother was in the car waiting for them. "What happened?" she asked.

"They were gone," Margaret said.

"Oh." Her mom looked surprised, but relieved, too. She squeezed Margaret's hand. "Tell me about it later," she said. "Dinner's in the oven. If we leave right now, it will be ready when we get home."

Chapter 29

Arthur didn't tell anyone about the trip to the valley, but he thought a lot about what happened there. He decided to write it in his book. He waited until Saturday morning, when the rest of the family slept late. He opened the closet door and went in.

He pushed through the row of clothes in the front and went back under the eaves. It was very cold. On a hook behind the coat hangers he found one of Margaret's old sweaters, a brown one with Popeye on the front. He put it on over his sleeper pajamas. He got the black crayon from the windowsill. That was when he noticed the picture.

It was an ice picture on the inner surface of the

storm window. Arthur had seen them before; they appeared in cold weather and were made of patches of frost and ice crystals. When he asked his mom, she said fairies made them. But he didn't believe in fairies.

This picture was special. The frost formed jagged peaks like mountains, and each peak was covered with tiny blossoms—the crystals themselves. Beyond the mountains was an oblong sphere made up of tiny drops of water: a lake, or perhaps a river. But this was the strangest part: There was a boat on it. The mast was another line of water, tall and thin. Beside it was the faint shadow of the sail, and the hull itself, shaped like a pointed shoe. Arthur stared. Why, that's the boat Christopher and I are going to sail on, he thought. Christopher said we'll sail around the world one day. And here's the boat to prove it.

He got to work on the story. He made his lines carefully: thick ones, curly ones, loops and squiggles. He told about the valley as it had been this time: the brown grass, the empty garden, the thicket in the pine grove. He told how Margaret had lied about the picture, and how Leon had lied, too. The grownups had been upset, and wanted to go home. He told how he had slipped away for a moment while they were talking. Looking back to make sure they weren't watching, he had trotted down the stream to the oak tree. He pulled the vines away from the base, searching for a present from Christopher. There wasn't a feather, or a pretty rock, or even a bit of bread with honey on it. At first he was disappointed. But then his fingers touched something. He looked again. There, drawn in the frozen dirt under the vines, was an arrow. It pointed toward the slopes that rose farther down the valley, where the mountains grew steeper and closer together. So that's the way they went, he thought. He took a stick and scratched the arrow out so no one else would see it. After all, it was his secret—his and Christopher's.

He stopped writing and examined his work. He added a dot, a backward loop. Here, at the part about the arrow, he drew a picture. Would he tell Margaret? He stood still, considering. Maybe, one day, if he felt like it. It was hard to say. He shivered. It was chilly in the closet, even with her sweater; and furthermore, he was hungry. He set the crayon back on the windowsill.

His stomach growled, and he left the closet, closing the door behind him. He thought he heard his mother getting up. He would like toast, he decided; toast and cereal and orange juice. He headed down the hall to let her know.

JANE LESLIE CONLY was born in Virginia and attended Smith College and the Writing Seminars Program at The Johns Hopkins University. Her first book, RACSO AND THE RATS OF NIMH, has won several prestigious distinctions and received rave reviews from teachers and children. Ms. Conly lives in Baltimore, Maryland, with her husband, Peter, her daughter, Eliza, and son, Will.

LEONARD LUBIN was born in Detroit, Michigan. He has illustrated many books for children, including Oscar Wilde's THE BIRTHDAY OF THE INFANTA, which won the American Book Award in 1980. He lives in Baltimore, Maryland.